THE CHILDREN
INTO A HYPNOTIC STATE

The Ch'Var known as Squick dabbed at Thomas's eyelid. An ancient iciness of Nebulonia leaped from Squick to the boy. Thomas shuddered as Nebulons slid around the eyelid into his eye, following labyrinthine passageways to the brain.

Squick held a glass container beneath the boy's eyes and caught the flow of luminous purple and yellow fluid. When the flow stopped, the Ch'Var sealed the container, slipped it into his pocket.

"Mr. Squick?" It was the boy's voice.

Damn! Squick thought, with a visceral, sinking sensation, knowing that this had never happened before. *I produced Nebulons, took his essence, and this boy should be in a coma . . . without his memories!*

Brian Herbert, son of Frank Herbert (*Dune*) and author of numerous novels, and Marie Landis, a first-time novelist, are cousins who met a few years ago after decades of separation. *Memorymakers* is their first collaboration.

SENSATIONAL SCIENCE FICTION

☐ **RATS AND GARGOYLES by Mary Gentle.** It is a city where the gods themselves dwell and where their lesser minions, the Rat Lords and Gargoyle Acolytes, have reduced humanity to slaves. (451066—$18.95)

☐ **ANCIENT LIGHT by Mary Gentle.** Lynne de Lisle Christie is back on Orthe, caught in a battle to obtain high-technology artifacts from a bygone civilization, while struggling to protect the people of Orthe from its destructive powers. but who will protect *her* from the perils of discovering alien secrets no human was ever meant to have? (450132—$5.95)

☐ **TIME OF THE FOX:** *The Time Warrior* #1 **by Matthew J. Costello.** Jim Tiber got the chance to break into the mysterious Red Building where physicists had created an experimental time machine. But another time machine was rewriting history, leaving Jim stranded in an ever-changing past, desperate to put Earth back on the proper time track ...

(450418—$4.50)

☐ **THE WAR YEARS 1:** *The Far Stars War*, **edited by Bill Fawcett.** A spine-tingling saga of battle in the skies featuring popular contemporary science fiction writers—David Drake, Todd Johnson, Jody Lynn Nye and others at their thrilling best. (450191—$3.95)

☐ **THE WAR YEARS 2:** *The Siege of Arista*, **edited by Bill Fawcett.** The high-tech far future war saga featuring science fiction's finest writers: Janet Morris, Christopher Stasheff, Steve Perry, Bill Deitz and more!

(450558—$4.50)

Buy them at your local bookstore or use this convenient coupon for ordering.

NEW AMERICAN LIBRARY
P.O. Box 999, Bergenfield, New Jersey 07621

Please send me the books I have checked above. I am enclosing $_____ (please add $1.00 to this order to cover postage and handling). Send check or money order—no cash or C.O.D.'s. Prices and numbers are subject to change without notice.

Name_____

Address_____

City _____ State _____ Zip Code _____
Allow 4-6 weeks for delivery.
This offer, prices and numbers are subject to change without notice.

To Jack Ryan –

MEMORYMAKERS

by
Brian Herbert
and Marie Landis

Brian Herbert

Marie Landis

ROC
A ROC BOOK

ROC
Published by the Penguin Group
Penguin Books USA Inc., 375 Hudson Street,
New York, New York 10014, U.S.A.
Penguin Books Ltd, 27 Wrights Lane,
London W8 5TZ, England
Penguin Books Australia Ltd, Ringwood,
Victoria, Australia
Penguin Books Canada Ltd, 2801 John Street,
Markham, Ontario, Canada L3R 1B4
Penguin Books (N.Z.) Ltd, 182-190 Wairau Road,
Auckland 10, New Zealand

Penguin Books Ltd, Registered Offices:
Harmondsworth, Middlesex, England

First published by Roc, an imprint of New American Library,
a division of Penguin Books USA Inc.

First Printing, July, 1991
10 9 8 7 6 5 4 3 2 1

Roc is a trademark of New American Library, a division of Penguin
Books USA Inc.

Printed in the United States of America

For Jan and Si,
with appreciation for
their patience and love.

PROLOGUE

Near the end of the last Ice Age:

Two muscular young men, members of the Ch'Var race, scaled the smooth sides of the ice cave, pulling themselves up on a sturdy ladder of corded mammoth hair. They carried minimal supplies—fat for the fire, dried fox meat to sustain them, and the most essential items, their killing weapons. One of them had a live, squirming animal strapped to his back.

The movements of both men were hurried, as though the pooled darkness below was about to overtake them.

"Faster . . . faster. Before the others waken," the man in the lead called to his companion-brother. "I'll have made my first kill before you reach the top of the ladder."

"I can't move any faster, fornicator of the dead," complained his brother. "I'm carrying the hound on my back. Or did you forget?"

The taller man forgave the insult. He could smell the slight fear his brother gave off, and he held a few lingering doubts of his own. Lordmother's Shaman would be angry if he discovered they were gone, and even more angry if he ever found out the reason for their departure. They planned to hunt Gweens by themselves and for the wrong reasons . . . reasons not approved by the tribe. There was another worry. The cold outside the warm cave swallowed life forces like a cruel enemy in battle. Still, he and his brother had agreed that too much time inside the cave during the long winter dark could soften a man and destroy his virility.

The taller man reached the outer rim of the cave, turned and hoisted his brother and the hound through the opening into a freezing blast of cold air. "The Ice Gods attack us," he said, "but at least we've left the stench of the tribe behind."

They hurried forward into the darkness and released the hound, one of the ferocious weasel-canines specially bred by Ch'Vars. The animal followed at their heels, his gait an undulating lope.

"He looks forward to the hunt," said the taller man and patted the creature's long snout. "Fresh Gweenmeat is what he needs. And so do we. The fox meat we carry is fit only for females and children. If we're lucky, our hound will find one of the ice nests Gweens build to protect themselves, and we'll dig them out and have a good meal."

"Gweens!" spat the other man. "No better than the scum on a pot of boiling fat."

"But good eating," reminded his brother. "Lordmother doesn't know everything. We gain the strength of our enemies when we eat them."

Despite the heavy fur and leather garments they wore, the Ch'Vars walked swiftly along the ice plains, their eyes glowing luminous red in the semidarkness. Eyes that could penetrate the darkness almost as well as the hound's.

"We won't need the stars to guide us home," said the taller man and handed his brother a small, flat object. "The stone-that-gives direction," he explained. "I stole it from the Shaman. He calls it magic and told me that Lordmother brought it with her from the stars. Ha! It's a tool, no different from other tools. He tries to deceive us but wastes his time. He ought to spray his foolish words on Gweens."

"Bad luck if we run into too many Gweens at one time," said his brother. He rubbed his hand vigorously across his eyebrows and dislodged a shower of ice crystals. "We could outwit them with words . . they are a stupid race of people with a simple language. Gweens have ceremonies for their dead, don't eat them in the practical way as we do. And they take but one mate at a time."

The hound stopped moving, lifted his head and sniffed the wind.

"He smells them," whispered the taller man and gave the animal a silent signal. Immediately it ran ahead, snuffling and snorting as it went. It stopped suddenly . . . on point.

The brothers followed the hound's line of sight. In the distance, across an endless sea of white, a small band of Gweenpeople trailed slowly toward the hunters.

"Three old men," the taller hunter said. "The rest are children." He knew the glow of his eyes could not be seen by the prey, for only Ch'Vars could see the tiny dancing lights within the eyes of their own kind. And he knew that Gweens could not pick up his scent. They lacked a fine sense of smell. With a fluid, practiced motion he removed his arrow gun from its sheath, loaded a projectile into the cradle of the weapon and cocked it.

His brother did the same and whispered, "The flesh of Gweenchildren is sweet. All the sweeter because Lordmother forbids it."

They exchanged smiles.

CHAPTER ONE

Ch'Vars and Gweens, these are the true
races of mankind. But only we know there
are two, and only we can distinguish one
race from the other—for Ch'Vars know the
secret of the Nebulons.

— From the Oral Tradition

It was the 14,312th anno of the Ch'Var calendar, and
for most other humans on Earth the middle of the
twenty-second century . . .

"Our race is waning, waning, dying!" Director
Jabu shouted. "What must we do? What?" The Director, a gargantuan dark-skinned man with a wild
black beard, was a flat image on the wallscreen of
Malcolm Squick's small second office.

Work harder, Squick thought, and as he thought
this, the words were chanted from a thousand unseen
voices.

Squick's second office lay beneath a first, reached
via a stealth-hidden passageway between the two. He
used this electronic corridor with only a cursory understanding of its mysterious workings, but this did
not disturb him. He had more substantive matters to
consider.

In the first office Squick was James Malcolm,
building manager for the Smith Corporation's branch
office in this locale, a branch that administered children's amusement parks. In the second office, Squick
was a Ch'Var fieldman, one of thousands around the
world networked to the Director on the confidential

radio-optic line over which the Director spoke at the moment.

Squick was a fieldman in a most unusual enterprise.

"The usual drivel," Squick muttered to himself. "Always another reason to increase our workload. Push, push, push . . ."

He heard sounds from the miniature lunchroom across the corridor—snapping, popping and slurping. He poked his head through the half-open doorway and saw his only non-robotic assistant, Peenchay, head bent over a gruesome meal.

"It's not noon yet," Squick said. "What are you doing in there? What are you eating?"

His assistant, a short, jowly man in a shiny yellow onesuit, looked up from the bloody flesh before him and grinned. "My snack," came the answer, a slow, menacing tone. Something pink-gray and wormy dribbled from his thick lips.

"Lordmother!" said Squick, and he forced his voice down to a whispered rasp. "You're at it again. How many times do you have to be told, forbidden? Can't you understand? One of these days the Director himself will pop in here and raise holy hell!"

Peenchay stared back blankly, and with a stubby finger he stuffed the wormy thing into his mouth and chewed.

"At least keep the damn door shut!" Squick howled, slamming it shut.

Squick returned to his office, but his thoughts remained elsewhere. A Ch'Var Inferior, Peenchay refused to take the powerful herbal drug prescribed for his kind to curb instinctual, atavistic cravings. Peenchay claimed he didn't feel well under the medication, that it slowed him down, didn't allow him to perform his tasks properly. A lie, Squick believed, but he had a genuine fear of his assistant and didn't want to press the issue.

This course of action exposed Squick to other dangers.

None of the fieldmen knew the location of Homaal, the Director's fortress, and he had an annoying habit of appearing unannounced to make spot checks. Jabu could appear in his full-dimensional self outside the lunchroom, by either of Squick's offices or out in the field that very day, or it might not happen for months, even years. It was a mode of travel Mother Ch'Var had used thousands of years earlier and passed on to her Directors, a mystical mode said to have nothing to do with the Inventing Corps. The unpredictability of travel was hard on Squick's nerves, and as he thought about it he wiped beads of sweat from his forehead.

Squick had his own transgressions to worry about, acts less messy than his assistant's but equally forbidden, equally punishable. He abhorred the behavior of his assistant but permitted it nonetheless, for reasons Squick didn't fully understand. This in effect made him an accomplice. And there was something more, a troublesome itch in his brain, a recurring thought that disgusted and frightened him.

Hurry up and eat, Peenchay, Squick thought, *and get the hell out of the lunchroom!*

Squick was miserable about the situation and saw himself as a captive, a victim of his own weaknesses and those of his assistant. He wished things could be different, and longed for happiness, for serenity. He lived in fear of discovery by authorities, Ch'Var or Gween. Authorities were nearly everywhere, it seemed, almost breathing upon him . . . forcing him into narrow, shadowy confines.

It could get worse, horribly worse, if he acted upon his disgusting thoughts, if he became more than a silent accomplice to Peenchay.

Squick felt a terrible corrosion growing within, an urging he had thus far kept in check. Or was it less than an urging? Might it be only a thought, a nagging, not so abnormal fear? Whatever it was didn't like to be examined, didn't make itself easily available to scrutiny. He was suspicious of it and envisioned himself slipping, slipping away, inevitably becoming worse than Peenchay. Squick vowed he would commit shittah first—that ritual suicide of his people, set in motion by the mind.

Shittah, shittah, shittah. I am born, I live, I die.

The fieldman saw himself in a downward spiral, with nothing breaking his fall except the safety net of conscience.

He wished Peenchay could at least learn to close the lunchroom door without a reminder. All Inferiors were stupid, but this one might be the dumbest of the dumb. "Every fieldman must have at least one Inferior as an assistant," the edict went . . . and edicts could not be questioned. Still, at least Squick understood Peenchay, could predict his behavior. The Director was another matter altogether.

Director Jabu's edicts came like mysterious comets from deep space. Paradigm: the one concerning his name. He had the full name of Jabu Karuthers-Smith, but despite his position (and his penchant for formality in other matters), he insisted upon being referred to as Director Jabu. It didn't fit, and constituted one of those frustrating bits of information that could not be researched. Every Director, it was said, had a mystical tendency, a tendency away from the hard edges of technology and toward things of flesh, of softness. The Directors were like Lordmother herself in that regard, and surrounding that vulnerable softness, that yolk and albumin jelly of living organism, was a thick, hard shell of gadgetry, of science—the Inventing Corps.

Squick's surroundings were dominated by the Inventing Corps, with stealth-encapsulations, wallscreens, radio-optics, and much more. There seemed no limit to the inventiveness of the Corps, and this suggested electronic surveillance of all field facilities, even of the lunchroom where Peenchay . . .

But Squick sensed other forces at work, powerful forces more akin to the Lordmother and her lineage of Directorships. These were the forces that prevented Ch'Vars from revealing the secrets of their race to non-Ch'Vars, and they were not of a technical nature. When all things were considered, Squick usually did not believe he was under surveillance, although at times this seemed like wishful thinking.

Hurry up in that lunchroom, dammit!

There must be so much money involved, Squick realized, though no more than personal compensation passed through his fingers, from Homaal. All the devices, the structures and the systems cost money. Lots of it. People needing the Service paid for it. But in the beginning there had been no money, only the filling of orders for people in need.

The Service had to do with mental health, Squick knew, primarily the mental health of Ch'Vars because of their fatal racial flaw—that high-strung propensity toward mental breakdown under the tiniest bit of stress. A mental breakdown that always triggered shittah.

Jabu's words hung in the background: ". . . waning, waning, dying . . ."

Mother Ch'Var had recognized the fatal flaw of her race early, and had identified the solution as well: extract happy, youthful memories (known as "embidiums") from Gween children and implant them in Ch'Vars. The Gweens were a happier, more carefree race, she had observed, and in any event the memories of happy Ch'Var children could not be used, since each extraction left a donor comotose, often near death. Only the strongest survived, and those few who returned to consciousness were mental infants, with no memories whatsoever.

Happy Ch'Var children could not be risked. There weren't enough of them.

The Lordmother lived in the time of no calendars. Money did not exist in those days, so in the beginning the Service was free. And even when money appeared, Directors succeeding Her did not charge for the Service but recognized it as a necessity, a right.

Maxim of the Lordmother: "Every Ch'Var has a right to life higher in priority than the right of Gweens, for Ch'Vars are the chosen breed. The best must survive."

Director Jabu held silence on the screen, and his expression of extreme displeasure seemed to indicate he knew the thoughts of some fieldmen had wandered. He expected undivided attention, and his wide eyes appeared to stare exclusively at Squick, boring right through him. As though he knew.

Director Jabu stood at a podium in a great ice-floored auditorium, gazing upon a throng of seated trainee fieldmen, all in variable-temperature white insulcoats like the cardinal red one he wore himself—those lightweight garments developed by the Inventing Corps that kept wearers comfortable in all temperatures.

He thought of Malcolm Squick, and in his mind's eye he saw the fieldman's personality, without a face, without physical features of any kind. Such a rebellious strain in Squick, like the untamed strain once in Jabu . . . but if that rebelliousness could be harnessed, could be channeled, Squick would make a remarkable Director.

It almost seemed incongruous, a rebel leading the race, adhering to age-old principles to continue

Ch'Var institutions . . . but it had always been so with Directors. They did not take orders easily. It was a balancing act, race leadership. Thus it had always been.

Someday Squick . . . or another . . . will stand here in my stead, gazing out into eternity, speaking the words that have always been spoken, thinking the thoughts that have always been thought.

The balancing act of personality. Walking the narrow line in new ways suitable to modern society. So many decisions that must be absolutely correct.

But this brain that I am, this linkage of thought and ideal to Lordmother Herself, this brain is not strongly logical. It is not supposed to be. A Director goes on instinct, following the path that seems appropriate.

It was a frightening task, an eternal quicksand of challenges that couldn't be considered in too much detail, for detail could interfere, could obscure. He walked an edge that wasn't an edge, on a line so fragile that it was forever crumbling away beneath his feet, forever forcing him to redirect, to re-attack.

I am the right side of our racial brain, he thought.

The left side, linked inextricably with the right, was the Inventing Corps.

The Corps had always been. It was Lordmother's defensive and offensive mechanism, developing ways of communication, of security, of efficiency. It emphasized logic, where Lordmother emphasized mysticism. It was the perfect complement to her strengths and weaknesses.

She was inspiration, the catalyst; the Inventing Corps was practicality, the application of her dreams, of her visions, the tempering of enthusiasm, the refining of it.

The enforced marriage of Lordmother and her Directors with the Inventing Corps was good because Lordmother said it was good. But Jabu was irritated by this. At times he wished he didn't have to work within the constraints of the Corps, but this thought seemed peculiar to him, almost ungraspable. For what constraints had the Corps imposed? Hadn't they provided this marvelous insulcoat that now kept him warm, broadened his security, even . . .

He sighed. His feelings boiled down to this: the very existence of the Inventing Corps was a constraint. Their existence limited his power, restricted his elbow room. Sometimes he wished he could begin from the Plateau of Now, from this place that Mother Ch'Var, her Directors and the Inventing Corps had brought the Ch'Var race. He wished he could go on without the Corps, but knew he could not.

Malcolm Squick, are you watching me now? Are you there? Or will it be someone else?

Jabu's monologue resumed, a fuzzy drone in Squick's ears. The fieldman squirmed in his chair, and out of the corner of his eye he saw Peenchay amble out of the lunchroom and head down the corridor.

Peenchay made dragging, scuffling sounds, and these were punctuated by the machinery noises of ceiling-mounted robot arms in the lunchroom, cleaning up where he had been.

"Hey, Peenchay!" Squick yelled, "whattaya think of the motto our Beloved Director came up with? What about it? 'Security, Efficiency, Lordmother's Way.' Kinda catchy, eh?''

I'm cracking, Squick thought. *Asking an Inferior for his opinion?*

He noticed a lull in the dragging and scuffling, and then it resumed, became louder.

Squick thought of the unprecedented mental health problems of his race, and blamed them on the complexities of modern life. Ch'Vars were inundating Lordmother's Way with embidium orders, and the frenzy to fill them was resulting in security problems . . . Gween police were sniffing around asking questions, forcing alternate methods of filling orders.

So much for the security part of the motto, Squick thought. *It's bending.* His gaze washed into the whiteness of the wall to one side of the wallscreen, and he heard only the drag-scuffle, drag-scuffle . . .

A shadow crossed Squick's teak desk, and he focused on the doorway. Peenchay stood there, a vacuous expression on his face. The Inferior's tongue slid across his lips.

"You called me, sir?" Peenchay's words were heavy, as if spoken through molasses. He was wet but clean, from a dousing by lunchroom cleanup equipment.

"Gweens are sensitive about their children," Squick said, "and when things happen to those children, they don't understand. Do you suppose this has something to do with their particular nature, with their overwhelming desire to keep their children happy?"

"Whuh?" Peenchay said.

"What if we pointed out to them that some embidium orders go to troubled Gween adults, as needed? Do you think it would matter?"

"Uh, I guess, gee, maybe . . ."

"Do you know where we get our embidium orders, Peenchay?"

"Uh, yeah, you get 'em."

"No, no, no! I *fill* orders. Like every other fieldman I make extractions and ship them to Jabu. Can't you remember that? Can't you remember anything?"

"I always remember to eat."

"Pay attention. Maybe if I repeat this often enough you'll get smarter. Maybe some of the important things will sink in."

The Inferior stared at him with intensity.

"Orders are developed through Ch'Var mental health specialists who've existed since the beginning of time—witch doctors, shamans, healers, bartenders, witches, warlocks, wizards, doctors of psychiatry, psychotherapists, preachers, priests, even prophets. Gween recipients are never told the source of therapy. It's said that Gween and Ch'Var recipients receive an herbal drug that erases certain specific embidium recollections—names from childhood, dates, addresses—any bits of data that could lead to trouble from Gween police." Squick paused and took a breath. "And I've heard that the herbals also meld the memories of the embidium implant with the adult memories of the recipient. I don't know this for certain, but I know drugs are used."

"I don't like drugs," Peenchay said.

"Right, right. Director Jabu makes the implants, or supervises them maybe, using techniques I don't know. He has a layer of secrecy and security around himself, a dimension of secrecy within the secrecy of the race itself. Oh, what's the use?"

It gets damn lonely here sometimes, Squick thought. *And the robots are even dumber that this guy.*

The fieldman's gaze slid back to the wallscreen, and his attention followed.

"Some of you have petitioned me," Jabu said, "asking why we cannot fill only Ch'Var orders. Why not discontinue the comparatively small number of implants in Gween adults, the petition asks, and thus make our lives easier? It goes on to suggest that we at least delay the filling of Gween orders in favor of our own people."

The Director's countenance became ferocious. "Our Blessed Mother Ch'Var began the practice of servicing Gween and Ch'Var alike, as needed. Orders have never been delayed intentionally or gone unfulfilled, and such horrors shall not begin under my stewardship!''

Squick hadn't originated the electronic petition; another fieldman had. But Squick *had* signed it. Now he tried to meet the gaze on the screen, but again the Director seemed to stare holes through him. Remarkable! Other fieldmen had commented on this phenomenon, the way they felt intimidated during motivational sessions, the way no untoward behavior seemed to escape Jabu's attention. It was said that Jabu, better than any Director preceding him, could sense things. He seemed to recognize minute, hidden psychological problems, unethical waverings and improper thoughts.

Peenchay said something, but Squick blocked it out.

The projection camera telescoped away from Jabu and revealed him in a magnificent cardinal red insulcoat, hood thrown back. In the foreground, over the throng of trainees, hung a thousand-tiered black ice chandelier, the black of Jabu's beard.

Rumor held that Jabu could drop the frozen fixture upon the heads of onlookers at a thought command, crushing them, and this had a great deal to do with the terror fieldmen felt in his presence. It had been instilled in them during training, and Jabu had methods of maintaining the condition.

Field equipment malfunctioned, sometimes killing fieldmen, and Squick believed these things did not happen by chance. Jabu claimed that only bad personnel suffered such mishaps, intimating that poor field decisions let to disaster . . . and he phrased his comments in ways that made many assume he played a direct role in the elimination process. Mishaps had a way of occurring shortly after unannounced inspections by the Director.

No one defied the Director. That would be sacrilege, a denial of all the Ch'Vars had been since the time of Lordmother, of all they represented in their separate evolutionary line. But Squick disliked the Director, thought at times he even despised him. What a challenge to conceal his feelings from such a man!

Peenchay spoke again, louder than before. "Uh, can I go? I got stuff to do. You know, things to shelve, things to straighten up in the van."

"Don't take the van anywhere," Squick said.

"Uh, I'm responsible for keeping it tuned. I need to test run it regularly to keep it in top running condition. That's my job."

"You're doing more than test driving it, Peenchay. I know where you're getting your . . . food. And I don't like it."

Peenchay stared at him stupidly, but in a way that frightened Squick. Something calculating there, and threatening, in a slow-witted way.

"It's just stuff I find lying around," Peenchay said.

He's using the van's coded memory disks, Squick thought, *going back over my daily trail before the comotose Gween bodies are found by others. Damn it, why don't I have the courage to . . .*

"Can I go now?" Peenchay asked.

"Yeah, yeah, get out of here."

The Inferior left.

Jabu's words and all other sounds slipped into the background. Squick concentrated on a little thought-pool of defiance. Despite all, it seemed to him that Director Jabu rather liked him, and since each Director handpicked his successor it amused Squick that he might be the one selected. There had been no overt indications from Jabu in this direction, and Squick guessed there had to be many other fieldmen higher on the ladder. But sometimes Squick fancied himself as the one in charge and speculated over decisions he might make.

Lordmother's Way had a curious organization chart—one Director in Homaal and all those fieldmen elsewhere, with no rankings between. They did have a large support group: Assistants (all Inferiors or robots), the brilliant Inventing Corps, Messengers, Maintenance Technicians, but none of them qualified to be fieldmen or Director.

Fieldmen were selected according to "Nebulon counts" in the body, and this had to do with a holistic mastery of the ancient power. But there were failings—the racial flaw—and like other fieldmen, Squick had received an embidium implant. Thus were the memories of another person, a Gweenchild, melded seamlessly with his own.

He often wondered about that child. Though the details of an implant donor were rarely discussed with the recipient, Squick had managed to learn from Jabu that the donor had been a boy, fifteen years old. Rather old for an embidium, and Squick wondered if some of his less happy memories belonged to the boy and not to himself.

Squick refocused on the mouth within the wild beard.

"We fill all orders because it has always been so. And when something has always been so, the future is clear!"

Behind Director Jabu the wall came alive in a spectacular array of color, then disintegrated to reveal an immense ice-encased computer screen that listed all outstanding orders. The frosty list scrolled endlessly. "Find the children we need!" Jabu said in a tone that sent chills through Squick's spine. "The happy ones!"

Squick experienced a rush of excitement despite his troublesome, nagging thoughts, despite his complicity in the acts of Peenchay. This was a shorter motivational session than any the fieldman could recall, but he felt no less motivated. If anything he felt a heightened sense of the moment, of his position in the history of his race.

The wallscreen went dark.

CHAPTER TWO

"We see things other people do not see, things other people can never see."
—Emily to her brother, in a dream

Squick stood beside his desk, touched a recessed button on the bottom edge of his belt. An oblong section of the floor separated and lifted him upward in a slowly spinning motion through an opening that appeared in the ceiling. The floor clicked into place above his lower office, and now he was in a tiny enclosure that at first glowed with bright white light.

Then a silent array of bright, sparking primary colors consumed him, traveled through his body and around, and he felt a pleasant, tingling sensation. This was a "stealth-lock," a place in a nether dimension that rearranged the molecules of his body, restoring them to Gween visibility. On an earlier pass-through in the other direction, the procedure had been reversed, removing his molecules and those of the articles with him from possible detection by Gween eyes or apparatus.

Now he went up again, spinning slowly through an opening in another ceiling, and presently he stood beside another desk in his building manager's office. Ostensibly, the level upon which he stood now was the second floor of the structure, a Gween-accessible area. One floor down was the lobby, and beneath that the stealth-encapsulated area that Gween technology could not penetrate. Neither could they penetrate the structural core that permitted secret travel between the roof and lower areas.

By design there were no windows in the Building Manager's office, only an array of wall weavings and Impressionist oil paintings, with a heavy door that led to outer offices. Gweens and Ch'Vars worked side by side in those offices, one of the unavoidable mergings of society that only Ch'Vars knew about. Ch'Vars tolerated it as they had to, despite all the problems associated with Gween limitations.

The pad on which Squick stood was connected to the doorlock mechanism, and his weight unlocked the door with a soft, nonmetallic snap. Some people in the outer offices referred to him as a mole because of his windowless office and the long periods he spent inside without emerging, but this didn't bother him. He found it amusing that he really was a mole, traveling hidden passageways most of them could never imagine.

In the hallway outside, a fat Ch'Var man in a blue suit greeted him—Lester Rumple, Branch Insurance Manager. Rumple gazed upon him with a look of slight suspicion, as he usually did, almost as if he suspected Squick was one of the legendary Ch'Var fieldmen. It was an unspoken, visceral thing. There were genetic reasons that Rumple, like other Ch'Vars, could not reveal racial secrets, and Squick thanked the Lordmother for this.

"Fire inspectors are due Monday," Rumple reported. (It was unsaid but understood that he meant Gween fire inspectors. Through an accident of social arrangement all inspectors and almost all firemen in the locale were Gweens.) "Something goofy with the fire and burglar alarm system," Rumple said, "so we'd better—"

"I know what's wrong," Squick interjected. "I'll take care of it."

Rumple went away humming the tune of a ditty familiar to all Ch'Var children, and the words surfaced in Squick's mind: *"With a Gween in your genes, there's no virus in your iris . . . With a virus in your iris, there's no Gween in your genes . . ."* He tried to shake the song from his thoughts.

The problem with the alarm system, Squick knew, had to do with a giant electronic eye in the lowest level of the encapsulated area, a secret sensor that protected the entire building. The device was ultrasensitive, so much so that it had to be recalibrated every few weeks. Usually Squick remembered and took care of the adjustment before the system went downhill, but recently he'd been too busy and the task had slipped from his mind. It was something Peenchay couldn't be trusted to do.

During inspections, Gween fire personnel saw only a phony alarm system, a front of standard-looking panel boxes and wires linked (unbeknownst to them) to the sensor. It had to be this way according to the Inventing Corps, and Squick's knowledge of the system didn't go very far.

" . . . With a virus in your iris . . ." Damn!

Sometimes Squick bribed the most susceptible inspectors, but in recent months there had been a change of personnel, and he needed intelligence reports before proceeding, reports that came from Jabu when they were ready.

Squick negotiated a short hallway of two turns, passed the odiferous public restrooms, and presently he was in a lobby filled with the unpleasant odor of unwashed Gweens. This was an old structure that had been extensively remodeled except for the lobby, which remained essentially unrestored: it had original brass fixtures and a tattered gray carpet that blew forth small dust clouds when walked upon.

The stench of the unwashed floated from a grocery store just to Squick's left, on the other side of

an ornate lobby archway. The store was frequented
by transients who purchased week-old loaves of
bread, cans of dog food and bottles of fortified wine
that were wrapped in brown paper bags. "Muscatel
Market," local office workers called it. As Squick
glanced inside, he saw the inevitable transaction occurring at the counter, where a female clerk in a
yellow apron waited on a teetering, drunken man.

There were other mercantile businesses fronting
the street, all subleased by the Smith Corporation—
a grubby French bakery adjacent to the grocery
store, then a shoe repairer and a crowded newsstand
that sold pornographic magazines and sensationalist
tabloids.

Squick stopped at the newsstand and waited in
line. Just ahead of him stood a man with a small
boy. These two had strikingly similar shapes from
behind, rather like pears of different sizes wearing
matching football jerseys identified by the team name
"Crushers." The child, no more than five years old,
Squick guessed, moved restlessly from foot to foot
and stared up at Squick with an expression of curiosity.

"Hi there," Squick said in his most pleasant, almost fatherly tone.

"Don't bother people, Bobby," the man said, and
when he turned, Squick could see that the man and
boy had nearly identical features—round and soft
with tiny, dark eyes—Gweens.

"Oh, he's no trouble," Squick responded. "Fine-
looking boy. Nice looking T-shirt he's wearing. I see
you're both Crusher fans. So am I." A lie, Squick
knew, but what the hell.

They struck up a conversation about two promis-
ing rookies the team had traded away. The Gween-
man seemed particularly agitated about this decision,
which he called stupid. Squick feigned agreement.
It was the only way to get along with Gweens.

The man only half smiled and said, "Maybe next year." He moved forward with the line.

As Squick stepped forward with the others, he thought, *Happy-looking boy, too. Good embidium material.*

He overheard the father and another man laughing about one of the headlines in the newspapers at the stand. Something about a race involving outhouses that had been converted into motor vehicles. Supposedly, the drivers sat on toilet seats.

Squick envied the easy camaraderie between Gweens, and tried to emulate it off and on.

When those ahead of him cleared out of the way, Squick purchased a copy of the *Financial Journal*, which he folded and put under his arm. Within minutes he was in his field van, searching for children.

Fieldman Squick took the van off automatic and turned the steering wheel hard to take a corner. He eased up on the accelerator. The van's motor ticked softly, a punctuated purr, and he watched a small blonde girl climb the ladder of a playground slide. She moved from shadow to sunlight, and her hair glistened enticingly.

From the pocket of his gray and black tweed jacket Squick removed an ornate wooden pipe carved in the shape of a Ch'Var hound, the long extinct weasel-like breed kept by his ancestors. Without lighting the pipe, he chewed nervously on the mouthpiece and surveyed the area.

It was a tiny park surrounded almost entirely by bushy trees and scrubs of laurel that cast broad morning shadows. There were warehouses on three sides and a row of small homes on the other, set in such a way that the play area was not readily visible from any home.

The child was alone.

Squick gunned the engine and roared over the curb

onto the grassy area of the park, toward the play equipment. A uramesh alloy shield snapped into place over the front bumper, and this low-slung, armored shield flattened a set of monkey bars as the van shot across the top of them. Then a rubber gripper on the end of a mechanical arm snatched the startled little girl from the bottom of the slide.

Several blocks away in a deserted industrial area, Squick touched a dashboard button, altering the color and license plate number of the van. Called a "chameleo-van" by the Inventing Corps, the vehicle was highly adaptable, and now it became maroon with a black top and luggage carrier. Another button provided the girl with a chocolate ice cream cone to keep her quiet.

He parked on a side street, spun around on his bucket seat and began interrogating her with ancient Ch'Var questions, using the hypnotic voice that had to be answered truthfully. These were the identical "Seven Sacred Questions" his people had asked Gweenchildren for thousands of years.

She was rather sweet, Squick thought, a happy young thing who seemed almost unafraid as she sat on the backseat licking ice cream.

He reached for her and stroked her hair. She smiled, and he withdrew his hand quickly, perhaps too quickly. As if overcompensating for this small physical connection and any possible meaning it might have.

Take the embidium, no more. The code of Ch'Var honor was strict.

I was only trying to show this child a last moment of kindness, he thought. *And not just to maintain the quality of her embidium.* He paused. *Am I kidding myself about this? Do I really feel tenderness? Lordmother, I sound like a hunter trying to avoid frightening the prey for fear of tainting the meat with adrenaline.*

He was a man on the edge of a precipice, with darkness below, and once again the terrible fear of what he might do, of what he might become, arose in his mind. And he was ashamed. Why did he have such nagging thoughts? Were they normal?

Gain control or commit shittah, Squick thought.

Shittah, though brought on by mental breakdown, aided Ch'Vars in problem times, facilitating a quick and painless end through the shittah death dance, culminating in a cessation of all bodily functions.

"Shittah is, in all things and all times, a comfort and a passage to the unknown."

In good times it was comforting to know that it was there to fall back upon as needed, a nest egg of mental strength. It comforted a Ch'Var in life, it comforted him in death. It transcended. It was the beauty within a broken thing.

As the captured girl spoke, Squick activated a hand-held transmitter, sending her answers to the Homaal data bank. When the ancient questions were complete, a tiny screen on the transmitter lit up, green letters on black: "Extract embidium. Fits 17 orders."

In the ancient way of his people, Squick gazed deeply into the girl's eyes, into the soft, easily penetrated surfaces there. And he spoke to her of wondrous things and wondrous people and wondrous places, so that her face filled with rapture. He told her an enchanting, magical tale, and immersed her so completely in the vision he painted before her eyes that she seemed to leave this place and this body.

The happiness Squick saw at times such as this made the rest of his task easier. She was no longer a child in a van on a dirty, deserted city street. She was a princess in an enchanted land, where nothing could harm her.

The girl's eyelids grew heavy, and a familiar sensation came over Squick—a yearning that suffused him with all the strength and purpose of his Ch'Var race. He was every one of his kind who had ever lived, fighting for survival in a torrential, soulless current of life. He shuddered.

With his fingertip he touched the tear ducts of his own eyes and felt an icy wetness that numbed his finger and fogged his vision. His fingertip sought an eyelid of the girl, and in a vision he saw her in the faraway magical land he had created for her. For the briefest of moments she smiled so sweetly, so innocently, in the way only a Gweenchild could do. Then she was immersed in a freezing storm of ice crystals that sealed her happiness and would not permit anything to taint it.

His vision cleared, and once again he was gazing upon a little girl in a van. She shuddered as Nebulons slid from Squick's fingertip into her eye. The viruses coursed the intricate, labyrinthine passageways to her brain, where they sought her memory core and vacuumed it away.

Squick withdrew his finger, then held a glass container beneath her eyes. And from her orbs flowed the bright purple and yellow liquid of her embidium, containing all of her childhood memories. It was a swirling, pungent-smelling mixture of these colors, with each hue retaining its integrity. The mixture was luminous, as if a light burned from each molecule, and it ran in such abundance that quickly it overflowed the container.

The girl's face lost vitality, and she slumped, but without falling from her seat. Carefully, to avoid contaminating the extraction, Squick sealed the container and packaged it for shipment to Director Jabu. Then he cleaned up the overflow and wiped the girl's face and eyes clean with a white, chemically treated cloth.

Moments later, the van's robot arm dumped a

limp, nearly lifeless form in the grass and weeds of a vacant lot.

As he backed his van away, Squick caught a brief glimpse of the child's silent body in his rearview mirror. "It's a lousy world," he muttered and suppressed speculation about the child's future. Nevertheless, he drove off feeling less than satisfied with this particular extraction.

Twenty-three minutes later, he pulled his vehicle into the parking garage of the condominium complex he called home and saw another condo owner, a Gween he had talked to a few times. He waved at the man and forced his mouth upward into a smile while his thoughts took a downward direction. *The guy's a jerk, but it's a good idea to keep on his good side. After all, he did give me that tip on the stock market. You never know when you need a favor from someone. It's the way life is—a series of favors given, favors taken. The objective is to get more than you give.*

"Going to the pool party tonight?" the man shouted. "It's a bring-your-own-bottle thing. Lots of goodies gonna be there, food and you-know-what."

"Maybe I will," answered Squick, though he entertained doubts about fraternizing too closely with Gweens, particularly this one. Since childhood Squick had made many Gween friends, but on his own terms. That had been particularly easy to do in his former residence, a duplex shared with an elderly lady. Now he lived in a complex that overflowed with amenities and Gweens. Gweens who wanted him to swim in the pool, dance in the dance room, exercise in the health room, play cards or billiards in the entertainment room. He'd only lived here a few weeks and so far had managed to maintain his privacy. Obviously that wouldn't last forever. Sooner or later he was going to have to socialize with the other tenants. Tonight was probably as good a time as ever. He groaned and punched the button for the elevator that would take him to his floor.

A pretty Gweenwoman stood inside, one who lived in his section of the complex. He'd noticed her long legs the day he'd moved in. Now he paid closer attention to the rest of her anatomy. Squick smiled, this time with sincerity. There was something exciting about Gweenwomen. Forbidden fruit, taboo stuff. He licked his lips nervously. You didn't marry a Gween, but that didn't mean you couldn't appreciate one. This one exuded the right pheromones, as the scientists put it, the proper chemistry to stimulate a response in the opposite sex—Gween or Ch'Var. "Hello there," he said. "Have you heard about the pool party tonight?"

"I've baked a cake for it," she answered in a little-girl voice and looked up at him with large, blue eyes. For a moment Squick saw in her features the face of the child he'd just dumped in an empty field. A small depression settled over him like a cloud, and he decided to skip the party. Anyway, tomorrow was going to be a long day, another extraction to make. Maybe more than one. This risk-taking was beginning to drain him. What if Gween authorities finally caught up with him?

Shittah loomed.

CHAPTER THREE

A Ch'Var cannot reveal the secrets of his
race. If he attempts to speak them, his
throat constricts and parches dry and hot so
that he is unable to utter a sound. If he attempts to write a secret, his arms and hands
cease functioning entirely. And when he
falls asleep the next time, as he must, a
form of shittah is set in motion. Secrets
have never been lost.
> —From a story
> told to Ch'Var children

In an elegant house near the condominium complex
where Squick lived, sunlight hit Emily Harvey's
green glass desk lamp and threw a shadow against
the wall. Above the shadow, ghostly, smokelike
shapes from the interaction of sunrays with bulb and
glass heat waves curled upward, as if the lamp were
afire. Such fine and delicate creatures those undulating nether forms seemed to be, Emily thought, as if
they had secret energies of their own.

It was the third day of Emily's Easter vacation, a
time for relaxation and thought gathering. But only
for a few minutes. Part of her attention waited for
the shrill cry from her stepmother that would call
her to the kitchen for chores.

The doorbell rang, and Emily found herself at the
front door gazing up at a pleasant-faced man in a
gray and black tweed jacket. He held a briefcase in

one hand and a peculiarly carved wooden pipe in the other. He tucked the pipe into a pocket.

His eyes glittered with excitement—they were dark, almost red. "Good afternoon, young lady. I have a gift for your family . . . free. No obligation to buy anything. Is your mother home?"

"I'll get . . . her," Emily said, thinking how false the word *mother* sounded.

She went to the kitchen, where her stepmother, Victoria, busily slammed unwashed dishes into a pile. The family had a live-in housekeeper, Mrs. Belfer, who didn't cook and refused to do much of anything in the kitchen. Emily had once estimated that Mrs. Belfer slept at least fourteen hours a day. Several times Emily had seen the housekeeper enter by the back door, paper bag in hand, a bottle of brandy or wine protruding from the top. Mrs. Belfer, a plump woman with fat cheeks, tiny hands and feet, and a great thirst, frequently poured herself drinks from the family liquor cabinet, though Emily had never heard her stepmother complain about this habit.

"Start filling the dishwasher," Victoria said the moment she saw Emily.

"A man to see you," Emily announced, her tone guarded. "Says he has a free gift for us." Long ago the girl had decided that no matter what she said to Victoria it would be wrong. It always was.

Victoria Harvey, a tall, well-developed brunette, held her body in the manner of a modeling-school graduate, at an angle with chin and hips thrust forward. Across one shoulder she wore a long, multicolored scarf which she pulled at nervously. Victoria's eyes were lavender, and she had perfect teeth behind perfect lips that smiled the perfect smile at everyone but Emily.

The perfect lips parted. "Couldn't you have said I wasn't in? I wish you'd use your head, if that's possible. You know I'm on my way to a fashion show. Free gift? I'll bet. Another salesman. I've told you a dozen times, I can't be bothered with them.''

Emily looked away, and her stepmother brushed past.

The stranger must have possessed charms beyond those of the average solicitor, because moments later Emily saw him seated on the living room couch with Victoria, engaged in lively discussion. Behind them a three-dimensional aquarium video showed tropical fish swimming silently through an underwater garden, and to one side a fireplace video crackled.

Victoria's stuff, Emily thought. *Artificial, like her.*

Emily had once dreamed that Victoria replaced her with a videotape, one that said, ''Yes, Victoria. Yes, Victoria,'' over and over again.

When they were younger, Emily and her brother, Thomas, had often eavesdropped from the hallway. Crouched behind a railing that separated the hall from the living room, they had watched their parents entertain guests—discussions of divorces, new cars, failed love affairs, marriages, stock options and land values, all stirred in a pudding of intriguing sound, with new words that had to be looked up. Today Emily could not resist the temptation to eavesdrop again, though it troubled her conscience just a little. What fascinated Victoria so much about this particular salesman, enough to make her late for the fashion show? It was almost a sacrilege for Victoria.

A large potted philodendron on the living room side of the railing partially concealed Emily from view. It was from this spot that she crouched and watched.

The man in the tweed coat smiled at Victoria. ''Thanks for giving me the opportunity to make my presentation, Mrs. Harvey.''

''Call me Victoria.''

''Such a lovely name. And I'm Malcolm Squick

of the Smith Corporation—catchy, isn't it? Squick of Smith. Our computer profile shows you have a birthday boy here, and we'd like to cater his party gratis. That means—"

"I know what it means!"

They exchanged smiles, and he glanced at an index card in his hand. "Thomas Harvey lives here, doesn't he?"

"How did you get his name?" Victoria asked. "Our phone's unlisted."

"Perfectly legitimate. There are lists for everything and everyone these days. You'd be surprised."

Mildly annoyed tone: "Still, it does seem . . ."

The salesman's smile broadened and seemed to disarm Victoria. She paused in mid-sentence and said, "You'll cater at no charge? Did Thomas win a contest?"

"It's the way we advertise our catering business— random selection of people, free services to a few."

Victoria placed a manicured finger against her lower lip. "Is it word-of-mouth advertising? We're supposed to tell our friends about you?"

"Exactly. Your son is quite fortunate."

Victoria smiled her perfect smile. "As you can see, I'm too young to have an almost eleven-year-old child. Thomas is my husband's son, not mine. And the older girl is his, too. I don't allow them to call me mother. It wouldn't be appropriate."

I'd never call you mother anyway, Emily thought.

Squick leaned toward Victoria. "To tell you the truth," he chuckled, "I thought the girl at the door was your younger sister."

Emily shook her head and grimaced.

Victoria caressed her hair with a well-manicured hand. To Emily she looked like a department store mannequin—and so did he. They appeared to pause in mid-sentence, mouths frozen open, with eyes that held no light. The vision frightened her.

Emily glanced away, and when she looked back, the mannequins had come back to life. "I see that Thomas's birthday is the Friday after next," Squick said.

"We plan to have the party on Saturday."

"That can be arranged, Victoria."

Squick's tone seemed insincere to Emily, and that crisp, toothy smile so similar to Victoria's. On the surface he looked distinguished and friendly, but there were nervous little twitches around the edges of the mouth and a hard stare to the dark, luminous eyes. Freezing coldness there that bothered Emily, the way they moved around and seemed to take everything in . . . the way they flitted toward the general area in which Emily concealed herself, as if he knew she was there.

She could almost hear those eyes, if such a thing were possible, grating in their sockets. Of course, she could never voice this thought, especially to Victoria. It would only provide the woman with another excuse to pounce and accuse Emily of having a sick, overactive imagination. And that tale would be carried to Emily's father, adding to it other stories of Emily's "mental problems," stories that forced Emily to see a therapist every other Thursday afternoon. Victoria had set that up rather neatly.

"What will you provide?" Victoria asked Squick.

"Everything. You needn't worry about a thing."

She'll love that, Emily thought, for their live-in housekeeper wouldn't be of much help. Mrs. Belfer hated parties about as much as she hated cooking. What an odd housekeeper, with less chores to do than Emily or Thomas. How could that be? Victoria never raised her voice to Mrs. Belfer, either, and it all added up to a puzzle that simmered inside Emily's mind.

Why had her father married Victoria? Couldn't he see beyond surface beauty to the evil beneath, to the plotting, vicious ways, to the lies and outright distortions? Apparently he could not. As Emily thought of this, she amused herself by envisioning Victoria fat, pimply and in a straitjacket. Fabulous, exquisite Victoria with monster zits glutting her face, zits that drove her insane. The picture made Emily feel better, though it changed nothing.

She stared for a moment at the wall nearest her and projected her own full-color image upon its surface. Though she crouched in the hallway, her image stood erect, a short, slim girl with only a few body curves, straight brown hair, a somewhat narrow face and oversized green eyes. The image was a recurrent trick of her mind that she didn't understand. She tried not to discuss it with anyone except her brother, who told her it must be a matter of physics. At an early age she had discovered that other people did not possess the same ability and could not see their own reflections on walls or sidewalks or sides of buildings. And since no one could see hers, it sounded crazy to mention it. Just as it was crazy to think she'd turned Victoria into a mannequin a few minutes earlier, or inundated her with pimples.

Despite her imaginings Emily felt like an adult caught in a child's body, a circumstance that made her essentially voiceless, unheeded in a world run by adults. She believed Victoria's inane chatter was listened to merely because of packaging.

In Emily's opinion the woman—she preferred to call Victoria "the woman"—spent a lot of time worrying about her appearance and nitpicking Emily and Thomas about every article of clothing they wore. As if that were the most important consideration in the world. And those little French words that Victoria scattered about like alms for the poor . . .

Emily felt anger building inside her. Something buzzed near her ear, and she swatted without seeing at what. The buzzing continued unabated.

Squick rose to his feet. "Good to talk with you, Victoria. Sorry to rush away, but I've a full schedule, lots of orders to fill." His voice lowered, to a weaving of silk: "I'll be in touch with you soon." He leaned toward Victoria, then straightened suddenly and walked to the door. "I'll see myself out."

Afterward, as Victoria returned to the kitchen, she hummed to herself. "Mmmm, isn't that nice. Now I don't have to worry about the arrangements."

Emily turned in the opposite direction, mimicking her stepmother under her breath. "Mmmm, isn't that nice—"

"Don't think I didn't notice you hiding in the hallway eavesdropping, Little Miss Crazy Brat!" Victoria called out in a ringing tone from the kitchen.

Emily wanted to scream back but held her temper and shut the door.

You're my bête noire, Emily thought, recalling a phrase from Victoria's French–English dictionary. She chastised herself for the thought and searched for an English alternative. *Bugbear, hate object, black beast. I like black beast. It has a riper, juicier sound. It rolls around on my tongue.*

Something clattered in the kitchen, an angry noise.

Birthdays were always hard on Emily. The birth mother of the Harvey children had died in an accident on Emily's fifth birthday. Emily wished she could enjoy birthdays the way other children did, but her therapist said it would take time, that one day she would no longer associate the day with death and it would come to signify life. It didn't seem possible.

The children were a comfort for each other. Through some magic that they generated between themselves, they obtained information neither of the adults in their lives would give them. The children often played a game they called Seek, an unusual playing activity that Thomas, a child prodigy, had invented when he was only two. It was a game the children felt might have disturbed adults, so they never discussed it in front of them.

During the game Emily would sit quietly on the floor of her bedroom with the door shut, while Thomas sat in a similar position inside his own room. Each would write a question to the other on a sheet of paper. And, without speaking, each would answer the question asked by the other.

Initially their questions had been simple. Emily might write, "What animal has stripes?" And Thomas, who could read and write at a fifth-grade level then, would scribble, "Zebra." The accuracy of their answers did not astound either child. Not then. It was, after all, only a game.

When their mother died, however, they searched their minds for the answers their father refused to give. That was when they played a new variation of Seek, one that frightened them into discontinuing the game. In their separate rooms each child asked what had happened to their mother, and then waited for an answer.

A few minutes later they compared notes. Both pieces of paper held the same statement, in the identical handwriting: "Mother died in a car crash at the intersection of 10th and Pine."

"She's not coming back," said Thomas, and he began to cry.

"I don't want to play the game anymore," Emily said. She placed her arms around her brother.

Three years later came the wedding between her father and Victoria, another dreaded day in Emily's life.

Emily envied her brother's carefree manner of looking at life, and sometimes she resented the good things that fell into his lap. Why hadn't the caterer discussed Emily's birthday? She would be fourteen in a month. Almost a woman.

* * *

That evening, Emily lay in bed and thought about the visitor to her house, particularly about the way his eyes, luminous and strange, grated in their sockets. Real or imagined? She couldn't tell.

In the quiet of night she heard another sound, a faint buzzing similar to the insect noise she'd heard earlier while eavesdropping from the hallway. Now the buzzing was much weaker, but it remained irritatingly present, as if deep within her ears and intransigent. She felt an eye-stinging, muscle-sapping fatigue, but her mind would not release its hold on her consciousness and permit sleep.

Low light filtered into the room from the edges of the drawn window shade and through her open door. Thomas, in his bedroom across the hall, had begun the familiar, neatly rounded rumbling that tugged him in a somnolent chain deep into his own private dream world. Talking in his sleep, probably. Emily heard only edges of sound, not words.

The buzzing faded.

Thomas didn't have nightmares, or at least he never spoke of any, and secretly Emily envied him. She thought again of the fancy catered party he would have. "Lucky Boy," she called him frequently, but only in her thoughts. She didn't wish him any ill will, didn't even want him to feel guilty for his good fortune. But often she wished that she might have just a little luck of her own to even things out. Why did she have to struggle so hard for the good things that happened to her? All head winds, it seemed, and no tail winds.

Something grated, like the stranger's eyeballs in their sockets, and Emily's heart went out of rhythm for a few seconds.

Light filled the room from the hallway, and she saw her father's silhouette in the doorway, identifiable in part from the way his long, curly hair puffed out at the temples.

"Still awake, Em?" he whispered.

"Yes, Daddy."

"I just got home. Had to work late tonight—open-heart surgery on an ex-baseball player. Rick Sewell. He was a pretty well-known pitcher in his day. Rifle Rick, they called him. He'll be okay."

"I'm glad."

Her father moved close by her bed, bringing with him a familiar antiseptic hospital scent. Dr. Patrick Harvey was a surgeon who frequently put in long hours for which he didn't receive extra pay. Quite often he attracted patients who didn't have medical insurance, and as a consequence he charged them only what they could afford, a circumstance that continually irritated Victoria. Lately he'd been talking about a sojourn in Mexico—he and other medical personnel would volunteer their services to peasants who couldn't afford doctors. He'd done this before in other countries, but this time he would be gone longer, several months perhaps.

This was one point of agreement between Emily and her stepmother. Emily wished her father didn't have to go on such trips. But Emily understood her father's need to perform humanitarian services, and she didn't think Victoria did. Victoria spoke in private to the children about how horrid it must be in such places, and insisted she'd never go to any of them because of the dirt and "all those diseased, animal-type people."

"They live in such ugly circumstances," Victoria said once. "What kind of a vacation would that be for me?"

Emily thought her father, a rugged, strong-chinned man with an oval face, the most handsome male she had ever seen. She paid little attention to the hole in one sleeve of his tan cashmere sweater or his mismatched socks, one blue and the other brown. But it concerned her that Victoria would nag him if she noticed.

Dr. Harvey knelt by the bed and kissed Emily on the cheek. "Victoria said you were disrespectful to her today."

"I wasn't!'

"She said you slammed your bedroom door."

"I didn't! At least I don't think I did. I was mad, but tried not to show it. The woman called me a name, so I went in my room to get away from her, to avoid an argument."

"She didn't mention that part."

"Little Miss Crazy Brat, that's what she called me. I didn't deserve it."

"I wish you could get along with her the way Thomas does. If only things could go smoother between you."

"I don't like her. Never will."

"Well, I know Victoria is difficult at times, but you've got to try, Em. You've both got to try." He shrugged his shoulders, said good night and left.

Exasperated with her father, Emily wondered why he couldn't see what she saw in Victoria—a fraud of a woman whose every pore oozed black bile. He was blinded by Victoria's charms, caught in the web of a finishing-school spider.

Emily curled into her blankets and closed her eyes. She drifted into a half sleep.

Just at the threshhold of sleep, a familiar visitor appeared. As always he came without announcement, a creature Emily never spoke of to anyone except Thomas.

The Chalk Man's arrival always followed the same pattern. The shadows in Emily's room would grow deeper and blacker and more threatening, and the creature would emerge from wherever it lived and begin to sketch itself.

She watched as the white-gloved hand appeared in

midair. Clenched in long, slender fingers, it held a large piece of white chalk which it moved soundlessly across the darkness, drawing a face, ears, eyes, nose and mouth. The mouth bothered Emily most. An oval of black edged in white, the mouth writhed and opened and closed with a chilling, high wail, like fingernails scraping slate. The words were unidentifiable.

Now the Chalk Man drew its torso, arms, legs and feet. More detail followed, with expert, artistic shadings. A rumpled white suit appeared with white shoes, and on the other hand, a white glove. Thus outfitted, the Chalk Man walked the blackboard of night, around and around the walls of Emily's room. Occasionally the thing smiled, and Emily wasn't sure she liked that either, though she guessed it was trying to be friendly. It didn't smile insincerely in the manner of the caterer-salesman, but she found something troubling there, something she could almost recognize, but not quite.

In a vague way the Chalk Man bore a crude resemblance to Emily's father—a similar oval face and white shoes like the golf casuals her father wore on Wednesdays and weekends.

The Chalk Man paused its restless march, stared at Emily with blackboard eyes. He reminded her of a snowman in outline form. She wondered if he was cold to the touch, and wasn't certain she wanted to find out.

Sometimes when Emily thought about the Chalk Man during daylight hours, when her thoughts were clear, it bothered her that the creature intruded on her private space, her dreams, her room. But it never harmed her and this time, as always, she drifted off to sleep.

CHAPTER FOUR

The Ch'Var who intermarries with a Gween
wastes the precious Ch'Var bloodline, for
the union of these races cannot produce
children. Ch'Vars with Ch'Vars; Gweens
with Gweens. Thus it has always been.
—Ancient saying

During breakfast the Harvey children listened half-
heartedly while Victoria lectured them about manners. The volume of the kitchen television was on
low, and the morning news flashed across the screen.
Whenever Victoria looked away, Emily turned the
volume up little by little. Something about a mysterious childhood ailment, and Emily wanted to hear
it.

"Turn that down," Victoria snapped after a while.
"I'm trying to tell you something."

When Emily complied, Thomas said, "I heard
buzzing, like I've been hearing all over the house.
Little flies or bees or mosquitoes, I don't know."

Emily nodded. "I hear it, too."

"You know what's weird, though?" Thomas said,
holding a piece of raspberry jam-smeared toast near
his mouth. "I haven't seen any bugs. Not one. It's
like they're moving around just out of sight."

Victoria glowered at Emily. "Now you've got your
brother imagining things."

"We're not imagining!" Emily said. "Listen! You
can hear them."

"You're both crazy!" Victoria said. But she grew quiet.

Now Emily heard the buzzing quite distinctly—a definite burr of sound. She tried to place its direction.

Her brother pointed at the back door. "Over there, I think."

Victoria arched her brows. "Nothing buzzing around here but your heads."

Thomas went to his lips with a finger. "Shhh!" he cautioned. He saw his stepmother's withering glance and closed his mouth, but only for a moment.

"An infestation of invisible insects!" Thomas said. "They got tired of being swatted and came up with a new breed. We've been studying about entomological selection in school."

"Ridiculous!" Victoria said. "No one's ever heard of invisible insects!"

"Doesn't make them impossible," Emily said. She spread peanut butter on a piece of fifty-grain toast, took a bite and chewed slowly. Anything to avoid the bowl of cereal Victoria had poured for her. Grown-up cereal tasted awful.

"I'm going to talk with your therapist about this, Emily," Victoria warned.

Therapist—the word bore dark connotations for Emily, as if anyone going to such a person had a straitjacket reserved. It was one of Emily's buttons that Victoria liked to push when Dad wasn't around, a provocation that boxed the teenager in. If Emily flared back, it would be distorted and described as craziness. And if Emily said nothing, her silence "proved" mental debility.

This time Emily smiled, and the maneuver disarmed her adversary.

Victoria looked away uneasily, then continued her lecture. "No time to discuss other subjects today. I have a tennis date in a few minutes and my hair appointment after that, and I need something new to wear before your dad and I take off this afternoon for the San Margarita Golf Tournament. You can't begin to understand the energy it takes to do all these things."

Emily stared at a cobweb on the ceiling.

"We'll be back tomorrow evening," Victoria said.

"If you won't be here, can we go see *Return of the Killer Couch?*" Thomas asked. "I hear it snuffs people with pillows."

"Nonna and P'no—P—oh, whatever. Your grandfather called, and he'll be by with Nonna this morning to take you somewhere."

"Great!" Thomas said.

Emily smiled.

"Stay home all day tomorrow and do as Mrs. Belfer says," Victoria said as she lit a white nicotine tube.

The children made long faces.

Victoria set the nicotine tube down in a ashtray and took a large spoonful of her fortified cereal. She alternated spoonfuls with nicotine puffs, and as she ate, smoke curled from her nostrils.

You look like a fire-breathing dragon, Emily thought.

Victoria pointed at Emily. "Do you realize that without manners or nice clothes a person is nothing . . . nobody? Look at you, Emily, uncombed hair and elbows on the table. Thomas, your T-shirt ought to go in the garbage. What people must be saying! This is a fine house, with a housekeeper, you know. Mrs. Belfer keeps everything nice and clean, and there you children are looking so nasty and dirty."

Nice and clean? Emily thought. The paucity of work Mrs. Belfer did wasn't done well, and now the house was infested with invisible insects.

"What's written on that shirt, Thomas?" Victoria asked.

"Tom-Tom the Atom Man," answered Thomas with good humor. He puffed out his chest to display. "Emily drew it because I'll be a microbiologist when I grow up." The shirt was white, with bright red, orange and yellow letters, each letter a smooth blending of color.

"You've made your brother look like a vagabond," Victoria said, taking a drag of nicotine. "You did it because you don't understand values, the importance of presentable behavior and appearance."

"People ought to feel relaxed at home," Emily protested. "Mrs. Belfer says so."

Victoria frowned. "Without nice clothes and your hair and nails done at the best salons—the necessities of the haut monde—life as an adult is very difficult."

"Daddy gets by without all that," Emily said, and with the words out she was afraid she had created trouble for her father.

Victoria's frown became a scowl, with deep lines that would have horrified her had she seen them. "Live in the proper neighborhood," she said tersely, "frequent the proper establishments, associate only with proper people." She took another drag on her nicotine tube.

"If you do all that, you can join the tennis club, right?" Emily said, her tone sarcastic.

"And what's wrong with that?" Victoria's eyes narrowed dangerously, her expression icy.

Emily stared at the television, which showed a female reporter in front of a hospital emergency-room entrance. Children were being wheeled in behind her.

On the screen, the reporter began her nightly news broadcast. Emily kept her eyes and her attention on the television monitor. Any news was better than Victoria's mouthings.

The reporter wore a strained expression as she spoke. "The mystery disease continues to strike children in this area. Joining us later tonight, county health officials will give us more information about what they believe is a new and virulent strain of an old disease—meningitis.

"The onset of the infection is abrupt, and young children appear to go directly into a coma. It is believed that adults are not susceptible because they may have developed immunity to a less dangerous strain earlier in their lives.

"Please stay tuned for further details."

"*Mon Dieu!*" shrieked Victoria.

Her shrill cry startled Emily. "What's the matter?"

"I've broken a fingernail on the edge of the table. Just what I needed. Now I'll have to see if I can get in the salon without an appointment. One problem after another!"

Emily stared at her stepmother's artificial lavender nails and saw one dangling like a broken talon.

"Turn that depressing news off, Emily," Victoria said as she carefully pulled away her broken nail fragment. "Well, I'm off now."

She stood, reached in her purse and withdrew a handful of money, which she gave to Thomas. "Buy yourselves some candy," she said. "The sugarless kind that won't rot your teeth. Before you leave, Emily, comb your hair, and Thomas, change your shirt."

Victoria slipped through the back door. Her body glided like a cat's, soundlessly.

"She never listens to anyone," complained Emily.

"She's all right" came her brother's cheerful reply, muffled by a mouthful of toast. "You just have to understand her."

"I don't want to," Emily said.

She heard the familiar whine of her grandparents' car outside, and dumped her cereal down the garbage disposal. Grandfather Harvey was lumbering up the front-porch steps when the children got there. He had bright green eyes and a thick thatched roof of white hair that hung over his forehead.

He hugged the children. "Ready to go? Nonna's in the car."

"Are we gonna have an adventure today, Panona?" Thomas asked, as they walked to the car. Panona was a name the boy selected, coined with *nonna*, the Italian word for grandmother. His grandfather didn't object, asserting that creativity should never be stifled.

"You bet," Panona promised.

"Where are we going?" Thomas asked.

"Exploring. So much to see in this world!"

Nonna, a tall woman in blue jeans and an oversized man's shirt, slipped the car's voice command unit over her mouth, and the rubber of it adhered to her skin. She spoke destination and speed commands into the unit. The vehicle accelerated and merged into traffic. With automatic controls activated, the steering wheel spun back and forth in front of her without being touched.

Emily sat in the front beside her grandmother, with Thomas and Panona in the back. It was warm in the car, and Emily touched a button to iris open the round window of her door. She looked up at her grandmother.

Nonna's hair was dark gray and her face covered with a fine web of wrinkles, but her eyes were childlike, large and dark. The sandals on her feet had been handcrafted from scraps of leather and wood into an elegant design. A turquoise Indian necklace hung around her neck like a collection of blue-green teeth, and on her hand a marvelous ring sparkled family history in each pearl, diamond and piece of gold. She looked slightly foreign.

Emily thought about values, of the things that were important to her.

"I like to drive manually," Nonna said when they were out of town. She removed the voice command unit from her mouth, slipped the device into a dashboard bracket and took the steering wheel in hand, her movements fluid. "Not in traffic, but out here on the highway to who-knows-where."

"Destination unknown," Panona said.

"Yippee!" Thomas squealed.

"A car is like a little nest," Nonna said. "Here we are, four birds all cozy and safe." She glanced at Emily and asked why she was frowning.

"Values. Victoria said we ought to get some."

Nonna arched an eyebrow. "I suppose she meant the qualities everyone should have. Honesty, compassion, a sense of responsibility. Things like that."

"She didn't mention those," Thomas said. "She talked about my T-shirt and Emily's hair." Thomas still wore the dreaded shirt, and Emily hadn't combed.

Signs along the road with black letters against white tempted and coaxed: "See the thunder beasts—five kilometers to the Jabu Smith Amusement Park." And then, farther along, another sign with a monster pictured on it and the words "Only one more kilometer."

In the distance Emily saw a giant statue at the side of the road.

The car slid to a stop by the statue, one of the thunder beasts, and the Harveys got out. The crude cement creature was massive, towering high overhead in bright sunlight at the park entrance. The ferocious head was beaded with small aggregate rocks, and the body of the statue, including its tail, extended a distance several times its height.

"Bal-u-chi-ther-ium." Nonna pronounced the word slowly, reading from a plaque. She wiped perspiration from her brow, for it was warm here. "Five meters high at its shoulder. Looks kinda like a giant pig, doesn't it? Or a bear."

"They were part of the explosion of mammals after the extinction of dinosaurs," Thomas said.

"That's right," Nonna said. "Thunder beasts lived after the Cretaceous period, in the Oligocene epoch. Get over here beside this one, children, and I'll snap your pictures."

As Nonna took photographs, she philosophized: "These big mammals pounded all over the country eating each other up, and now they're gone like their predecessors. What are we left with today? Corporations that eat each other up." She laughed, a rich and full musical sound.

"Victoria says you're a leftover hippie like they used to have a long time ago," Emily said, staring at the turquoise Indian necklace her grandmother wore.

A snort erupted from the old woman. "She insults me. I'm too young to have belonged to that period of history. But I write poetry and make my own shoes and I was born in another country. So I'm offbeat in your stepmother's eyes, I suppose." Nonna sighed. "I don't need to impress anyone. It's a waste of good living time."

Nonna might be her father's mother, but she didn't look or act like him, Emily decided. Both were tall and oval-faced, but there the resemblance ended. Her father never discussed much with Emily or Thomas.

Once he had told Emily that she reminded him of her grandmother. "You have a lot of the same qualities," he'd said with a grin. "A little odd, but very, very . . . special."

Emily was flattered.

The children and their grandparents took a path

that led to the forest and found other beasts hidden in the shade, animals that peered around trees and leaves and nestled in the midst of ivy, wild berries and ferns. Saber-toothed tigers known as smilodans, silent and unmoving, inhabited the sweet-smelling wilderness, and Emily saw a creature that looked like a giant armadillo with a lethal barbed ball on the end of its tail. Another hung from a cement ledge and grinned at them with eight-inch teeth. Thomas pulled forth an imaginary sword and defended Emily against imaginary attack.

"Pow, pow, pow," he said, flailing at the air like Quixote.

Emily watched her brother. He had a vivid imagination himself, and his favorite game was called "What If." What if aliens from another world landed in their backyard? What if you could turn mashed potatoes into ice cream? What if Emily's Chalk Man was real?

"Those are all done for," Thomas shouted, and he ran ahead to join his grandparents, the baby fat jiggling around his waist as he moved.

On one side of the path, a few meters to the left of Emily, the arched back of another cement thunder beast loomed high in the air. This animal was larger and more menacing than any of the others she had seen.

Ahead of her, Thomas and the grandparents rounded a corner and disappeared from view. Emily looked behind her, saw no one else on the path. There were noises around her, birds singing and the rustling of leaves, but these sounds grew muted and faraway, like notes of music carried off by the wind. A shiver of fear rippled along Emily's spine, and she hurried to catch up with her family. According to signs, the path only led in one direction—straight to the exit. When she decided she was safely past the creature that had disturbed her, she slowed her pace and thought how foolish it was to fear something made of cement.

A surprisingly cold breeze suddenly caught her hair and lifted it, slapping it painfully against her face. The cold became a freezing blast that crept beneath the collar of her dress and chilled her to the core. Emily moved to escape it, but the breeze intensified to a ferocious, howling creature that pummeled her body with fists of ice. Tears of pain filled her eyes, and she attempted to run, but the wind blocked her. A shower of evergreen needles roared across her head, scratching her painfully and filling the air with a sharp smell of spice.

"Help me!" she cried, her eyes closed.

But no answer came.

Emily was pushed backward. She stumbled, inhaled air with sharp, pain-fused gasps and tried to shout again. Terror thickened her voice and only a mumble of sound escaped her lips.

Then as suddenly as it had begun, the wind whispered itself away and the woods were silent once more.

Directly in Emily's path stood the huge, snouted beast she thought she'd left behind, its back arched in an angry curve. Sharp teeth protruded from its half-open, underslung jaw. Emily stood mesmerized, and desperate thoughts fought their way into her mind.

You're not here! she thought. *Go away!*

The folds of the monster's skin, the sheen of its horns and the glisten of its tiny pig eyes all seemed lifelike. Beads of saliva dribbled from its mouth, and she thought she saw its eyes flicker. When she looked closer, the eyes became flat and unblinking. Dead eyes. Eyes of stone.

"You're only cement!" she shouted. "You can't run or make noises or eat. You can't eat me!"

The animal vanished from her path.

Emily looked back through a filtering of trees, and saw the snouted beast statue on the side of the path, exactly where it belonged, its back arched above the underbrush. She stared at the animal, and it stared back without expression.

"I'm dumb," she said. "Dumb, dumb . . ."

Victoria's criticisms flashed through her mind, hostile whisperings. "Little Miss Crazy Brat."

Moisture dripped from the beast's mouth, and Emily's throat tightened. She thought she detected a small movement of its jaws, a minute trembling, and she suppressed a scream.

"You're a statue . . . a statue," she repeated to herself as she turned to leave. Fortified by these words, she walked briskly along the path, somewhat comforted. Until she heard a sound behind her, slow and thudding, gaining on her.

She ran. And bumped into Thomas at the exit.

"I thought something was after me!" Emily wailed. "There was a wind and . . ." She let her tears flow, with great, heaving sobs.

Thomas put his arms around her and held her until she grew quiet. "You're okay now," he said.

"Sometimes you seem older than I am," Emily said.

"Not just because I'm bigger? For other reasons, you mean?"

"For other reasons."

They rejoined their grandparents and walked back to the car.

"This amusement park is getting an old-fashioned merry-go-round," Panona said. "I read that Jabu Smith is bringing in a real antique with wood carvings you don't see everyday. People don't do much of that anymore. Takes too much patience and time."

"Someday the last craftsman will die," Nonna said. "Then what?"

"Hats off to Jabu Smith and people like him," Panona said.

They drove down the highway to an oceanside eatery that advertised kilometer-high hamburgers and ice cream cones as big as Antarctica.

On wooden tables outside, they spread a plethora of food in the bright sunlight, and Emily and Thomas began gorging themselves.

An ocean breeze wrapped around Emily, a perfect, warm breeze that caressed her and soothed her from the harshness of the other wind.

"Smell the flowers in the air," Nonna said, "all mixed with briny odors from the ocean. It's the wind blowing petals from a tropical paradise, bringing perfume from faraway."

"The wind is sharing its bounty," Thomas said with his mouth full.

"One day you'll write poetry, young man," Nonna remarked. "Same as I do, but more cheerful, from the happiness in your heart." She gave Emily a hug. "And you, dear one, will wear a rainbow. I wish . . . Well, it doesn't matter what old folks wish."

"Wish what?" Thomas asked. He was always the curious one.

"That life gives you the best of everything," laughed Nonna. "And more selfish things. I'd like to steal you from Victoria and your dad so I can see you every day."

"I'd like that," Thomas said with enthusiasm. "We could always go home for visits."

Emily was without words, and she pressed snugly against her grandmother's bosom.

When they returned to the Harvey home just before dark, Victoria and their father were still on their trip.

"Don't forget Mrs. Belfer is here," Emily said.

"The one who sleeps," Nonna said with an edge

to her voice. "I don't think I've exchanged ten words with her."

"We'll be fine," Thomas said.

They kissed each other goodbye, and the children entered the house.

Moments later, the doorbell rang, and Emily peered through the window by the door.

"It's a man," she whispered to Thomas. "The salesman who was here yesterday."

CHAPTER FIVE

> Our race is winding down, melting into the soil. I see it in diminishing population and Nebulon counts, and I feel it in my bones . . . racial shittah!
>
> —"The Frozen Journal of Jabu"

Malcolm Squick saw the brown-haired girl at the window by the front door, peering around the curtains. He smiled at her, knew from the amoeba-cams he'd left that she and her brother were alone, except for the alcoholic housekeeper, asleep in her room off the back porch.

The drunken sot would not interfere.

A screen from Squick's training flashed in his mind, with frost around the lettering, just as he had seen it in the great ice auditorium of Homaal:

Amoeba-cams: living radio-optic organisms stealth-encapsulated so they occupy a wavelength of light invisible to Gweens. They buzz, but only within a sound range beyond the auditory perception of the target race. When released in a structure by a fieldman, the amoeba-cam divides into the number of rooms and hallways, providing visual and auditory sensors in each.

Squick had released an amoeba-cam here the day before.

"Flies on the wall," Director Jabu called them.

With these remarkable devices from Jabu's Inventing Corps, fieldmen knew when adults were home so that calls could be made upon unattended children. If adults appeared suddenly, there were deadly contingency plans.

"Remember me? I was here yesterday," Squick said loudly enough so that the girl could hear him through the glass. "I forgot to ask a couple of things." He lifted his briefcase.

"Our parents aren't here," Emily shouted back.

"You're Emily, aren't you?"

No response. She gripped her lower lip in her teeth as if afraid, then released it.

A boy appeared beside the girl, obviously younger than she but taller, with curly dark hair and similar features. Even through the glass Squick could see that the irises of both children lacked the pale red glow of Nebulons that characterized the eyes of the Ch'Var race, confirmation to him that these were Gweenchildren, target children. Only Ch'Vars could see the luminosity in Ch'Var eyes.

"Ah, this must be the birthday boy!" Squick exclaimed loudly. He popped open his briefcase without putting it down, removed several colorful party hats. "Which would you prefer? What about cookies? And games? Which games do you want to play?" He held up a red and black party favor for them to see.

The girl scowled, but the boy disappeared from the window and opened the door. "I'm Thomas Harvey. I like the blue hat, the one with the yellow clowns."

"May I step inside for a moment? I have several selections to show you . . . even sample cake and ice cream flavors!" Squick bubbled with feigned excitement. He saw Emily Harvey behind the boy, near the doorway to the living room, her small, pretty face pinched in disapproval. A more difficult child to convince than her brother.

Thomas looked at his sister. "Is it okay?"

"I don't have much time," Squick said with urgent cheer. "So many orders to fill!"

"All right," answered a hesitant Emily. "We're not supposed to let in strangers, but if it's for the party . . . well, I guess . . ."

Squick assumed his most benign expression. "I'm not a stranger. Your mother and I had a nice conversation yesterday."

"She's not our mother," Emily answered. "She doesn't like us to use that word."

As she let the caterer in, Emily recalled Mrs. Belfer's statement that the only safe males in the world were under twelve years of age and puny. Mrs. Belfer commented often that she hated men and had no interest in them, but Emily suspected otherwise. Once, when the intercom didn't operate, Victoria had sent Emily to Mrs. Belfer's room. The housekeeper's quarters were crowded with heart-shaped lace pillows, and scattered across her bed were assorted paperback books with lush, juicy titles such as *Golden Passions, Island of Desires,* and *The Lust of Louise.*

It was best to let the salesman in. If Victoria had asked the man to stop by and talk to Thomas and Emily refused to answer the door, Emily didn't want to think about the consequences.

With a briefcase, conservative dark suit, white shirt and sedate tie, the caterer resembled a banker or an accountant. One pocket of his suit bulged a little, and Emily recalled the peculiar pipe he had stuffed into his tweed jacket the day before. The pipe had a little animal face like a weasel, with ferocious eyes. It seemed clearer to her now than when she had actually been looking at it.

"I'm Mr. Squick," he said, and latched his briefcase.

"Our housekeeper could talk with you," Emily said. "But I'd rather not disturb her."

"Mrs. Belfer goes to bed early," Thomas said. "She's old—forty-seven, I think. She wears a red wig that slides around on her head when she walks, and you can see darkish hair under it."

"I don't want to waken her," Squick answered, and he stepped inside and closed the door.

The house changed.

Emily wondered if Thomas felt it. An odd sensation, as though something had been shuffled about, moved from its familiar position. The feeling was ice-cold and prickled the back of her neck. She looked about the hallway and saw everything in its proper place: the narrow bench with coat hooks on it, the pickle-finish side table with a Tiffany lamp, the paintings to each side on the walls. Still, the agitation on Emily's neck remained. The order of the house had been disturbed.

"I'm afraid we won't be of much help to you," she said.

Squick moved a little closer to the children. "Oh, but you will! So many details you can help with. You want to participate in the party, too, don't you, Emily?" He looked at the boy and added, "Say, that's a great T-shirt. Mind if I call you Tom-Tom? It's easier to talk to someone when you know their nickname." He patted Thomas's cheek.

"Emily printed it," said Thomas. "With a waterproof marking pen. Our stepmom hates this shirt."

"I see you're wearing it anyway."

Thomas beamed.

"It's the way children assert independence," Squick said. "A necessary step."

Thomas's smile weakened. He looked puzzled.

"Adults always want you to do things their way, right?" Squick asked. "Never realizing you've got a mind of your own." He paused a moment. "I'd

like to see your room, Tom-Tom. It will reveal the
things you like, give me ideas for the entertainment.
All right?''

''Okay,'' Thomas said, and led the way down the
hallway to his room.

As Emily followed, she recalled that long ago she
had decided Thomas had the disposition of a puppy.
He loved everyone, trusted people too much. Like
he'd trusted his friend Booger, a boy who picked his
nose in class and drew realistic skulls on his fore-
arms in red ink. Booger was a square-faced boy who
wore his hair parted in two places. He smashed Thomas's toys, the toys that Thomas shared with him,
because Booger enjoyed smashing things. Toys or
people, it made little difference to Booger.

Her brother could calculate complicated mathe-
matical problems, could read and understand his
father's medical journals and once, when he was five,
he had constructed his own steam engine. But sometimes he couldn't see things, things that were obvious to Emily. This Squick was a question mark, and
Emily hadn't quite made up her mind about him.

Upon entering the bedroom, Squick shook his
head slowly from side to side. ''Funny the things
adults demand of kids, wouldn't you say? Most children tell me their parents deny them their rights.''

Emily watched her brother show Squick his space
books and science fiction anthologies, and thought
how extraordinarily odd the man's comments were.
She didn't like the easy familiarity of this caterer-
salesman, or the fact that he called her brother Tom-
Tom. It sounded too intimate, almost perverse. But
good manners prevailed, and she made no comment.

Squick sat on the bed, briefcase open on his lap.

Emily cleared her throat and her voice rose. ''I
was just wondering: How did you know my name?''

''From computer files on our clients. Not enough

information on file, though. That's why I'm here to-day.''

"But it's not my party."

"You'll be there, I presume, and as the birthday boy's sister you'll occupy a very important position.''

"Victoria might not like that," Emily said.

"I'll discuss it with her," Squick said. "She shouldn't ignore your role.''

"You'd do that?" Emily asked.

"I would.''

For the moment he seemed like a nice man to Emily, one who saw through Victoria. Emily stared at the samples in his briefcase without focusing on them. "Would you like a cup of coffee?" she asked with a smile. "Or a cold drink?''

"Coffee's fine. Black please." Squick returned her smile. It was the toothy smile she'd thought insincere the day before. Now it seemed different.

"It'll take me awhile," she apologized.

"Don't rush," Squick said.

When she was gone, Squick asked the Seven Sacred Questions, firing them at Thomas in the hypnotic Ch'Var voice that had to be answered truthfully. Squick ran through them quickly. He asked for the boy's happiest and saddest memories, whether he looked forward to each day, what he enjoyed doing most, what he thought of the people closest to him, what the best or worst things were about being alive, and whether he was afraid of anything or anyone.

Thomas's answers came without hesitation and were concise, as required by the voice. They revealed to Squick's trained ears that the boy had a positive outlook about the world and that he got along well with people around him, even with a stepmother who apparently could be difficult at times. The boy's saddest memories concerned the loss of his mother. No longer could he remember her face, and this bothered Thomas a little. But these feelings were not enough to disqualify the child, since he had overcome them to a remarkable degree.

All answers went into the hand-held radio-optic transmitter and presently the screen read: "Embidium fits 32 orders. Extract."

I'll take the girl's, too, Squick thought, *without questions. She seems happy.*

Squick had done this before—extracted childhood memories on intuition without the Seven Sacred Questions. Such decisions involved an inherent risk, he knew, but thus far he'd made no mistakes.

Jabu spoke of this on occasion to all fieldmen, however, hammering home the importance of following proper procedure. "Procedures are for a purpose" was his mantra. "Only employ your Nebulons after following prescribed steps. Nebulons must not be wasted!"

Once used for embidium extractions, the viruslike organisms could not be reused. They had but one function, Squick realized.

Of course, the holistically healthy Ch'Var body produced replacement Nebulons all of the time, especially in Squick's body. If anyone could afford to waste a Nebulon, it was Malcolm Squick, fieldman extraordinaire. His rare physical prowess when it came to Nebulons bolstered him and diminished his fear of Jabu's wrath.

The necessity of filling orders was instinctual in the Ch'Var race, and virtually nothing could interfere with the drive for completion. The fulfilling of an order was a satisfying experience, almost sexual in its intensity.

When Emily returned with a steaming mug of coffee, she saw Squick slip a small black device into his inside jacket pocket. She didn't give it much thought, deciding it was probably a calculator, and set the mug on the nightstand.

Squick spread his wares on the bed: party favors, balloons and samples of food wrapped in elegant little packages. He opened a large book of photos, displaying a variety of birthday cakes, some in the shape of thunder beasts, some formed to look like clowns or acrobats or animal trainers, even one that looked like a spaceship. The colors of the creations ranged from an unusual yellow-green to deep violet-blue—entrancing hues with lambent rays of light that reflected firelike against the underside of Squick's chin.

Emily didn't like the thunder beast cakes and was glad when Squick turned the page so she couldn't see them.

"Let me see," Squick said. "You'll be eleven, Tom-Tom. What about this for your tablecloth?" He brought forth a length of deep blue fabric, as a magician might pull an object from a hat. Silver stars glittered on its surface, glinting like suns in distant space, flickering and fading and flickering again.

"Weird," Thomas exclaimed. "I like that one."

"I thought you would."

Squick began a monologue about his wares and services that filled the room with words. Words spilled down the hallway into the farthest corners of the house, and Emily began to feel drowsy. She sat on the carpet and watched Squick's mouth, the incredible gyrations of his perfect lips. And she watched his eyes, the luminous, almost red eyes that made little clicking sounds when he blinked.

Thomas sat on the bed beside the array of wares, seemingly too many things to have come from one briefcase. He fingered a party favor, looked up, frowned and said, "I hear buzzing again."

This child hears an amoeba-cam? Squick could hear the buzzing of stealth transmitters distinctly;

one was in the corner of this very room, identifiable to his Ch'Var eyes as a pale red glow. He hadn't studied the amoeba-cam reports on this household thoroughly, but recalled the conversations between the children about buzzing noises. Could it mean both children heard the secret frequency? It didn't seem possible.

The fieldman stared into Thomas's eyes. Detecting no Nebulon luminescence there, he reconfirmed this was not a Ch'Var child. It must be something else the boy referred to, though Squick heard no other buzzing. Might it be a different sound, one that only Gweens could hear?

Squick's monologue continued, and Emily tried to focus her attention on it. His hypnotic words might have been mouthed by an alien, but she felt she understood chunks of thought, concepts of great significance. Yet if someone had asked her to explain his words at this moment, she would have been helpless to do so. They were a blur. Her head felt excessively large for her body, and she had a strong desire for sleep.

With his mouth turned in a foolish grin, Thomas said, "Odd-to-the-mega. My head feels like a watermelon. I think you put too much stuff in there, Mr. Squick."

As Squick gazed upon the boy, he felt a familiar sensation coming over him—the hoary yearning that could not be denied. The boy's eyelids were heavy, and he appeared ready to fall asleep. Squick shuddered, touched the tear duct of his own eye with a forefinger and felt icy fluid flow from the duct to the tip of the finger.

Nebulons! he thought, unable to restrain his joy. It was always like this, a feeling of rampant ecstasy at the accomplishment. Squick couldn't imagine his life without the ability, and feared the mundane existence suffered by so many impotent Ch'Vars.

I am fortunate indeed, he thought.

He dabbed the boy's right eyelid with a cold, wet fingertip. An ancient iciness of Nebulonia leaped from the fieldman to the boy, linking Squick with the glory and dimming hopes of the Ch'Var race. The subject shuddered as Nebulons slid around the eyelid into his eye, following labyrinthine passageways to the brain. Squick almost whispered the explanation—*Nebulons, clever viruses seeking memory cells, embracing them and vacuuming them away.*

Squick's fingertip was warm now, and for a moment he looked away, toward the girl. Her eyelids were as leaded as her brother's, and she struggled to keep her head upright.

The Ch'Var fieldman withdrew his fingertip, then held a glass container beneath the boy's eyes and caught the flow of luminous purple and yellow fluid. When the flow stopped, Squick sealed the container and slipped it into his pocket.

He felt extinction beckoning, wondered if his Nebulon count would hold, if like the great ones he would keep it through very old age. Some lost it in their early or middle years, fading away or dropping off suddenly. Some never had it. There was no identifiable pattern. Sometimes people lived almost an entire lifetime without a solitary Nebulon, and inexplicably developed high counts in later years. So for brief periods the very old became teetering fieldman, taking extractions from Gweenchildren.

Flames before death.

"Mr. Squick?" A boy's voice.

Squick came to awareness, saw the boy gazing up at him. A little unwiped fluid remained on the boy's cheeks, which he wiped away himself with one hand.

"You okay, Mr. Squick?" Thomas asked.

Damn! Squick thought with a visceral sinking sensation. *I produced Nebulons, took an embidium, and this boy should be in a coma . . . without his memories!*

Perplexed and terrified, Squick removed the glass container from his jacket pocket. The container was full of swirling purple and yellow fluid, and he flipped open its lid, immersing his wet finger in the tepid liquid.

The solution clouded momentarily, indicating positively that the extraction had been made. But the boy continued to look at him. How? The girl stared, too, though she should have remained hypnotized from the words that filled all voids.

"Your name?" Squick asked, looking intensely at the boy.

"Thomas Harvey, sir. But you already know that. Are you all right?"

"I'm fine, fine."

Squick fumbled with the glass container, closed it and slipped it into a padded briefcase slot beside similar containers, some of which were empty and some of which had fluid in them.

"What are you doing?" Emily asked.

Squick thought quickly. "Special things."

He brought forth a large piece of white tissue, and with it removed from another briefcase slot what looked like a piece of unwrapped red candy.

"Ver-r-ry special stuff," Squick purred. "This candy is so special and so delicate, I don't want to alter the flavor or aroma with chemicals from my skin."

He extended the candy toward Thomas. "Smell this, Tom-Tom, and see if you want it at your party. It's called scent-candy. You don't eat it, you smell it. The nose and taste buds have a close affinity, as you must know from reading science. Lose one sense and you can lose another. This treat provides more joys than candy taken into the body the conventional way.''

He held it under Thomas's nose.

''It's different,'' Thomas said. ''I like it. Lots of flavor.''

''And you?'' Before Emily could react, Squick knelt over her and let her smell the fullness of the candy, the most intensely sweet and delicious odor of ripe strawberries in her experience. Squick's eyes became the red of the berries as they stared into hers, invading her, almost caressing her.

Emily could not tell hours from minutes. Somewhere she lay in deepest sleep, and something touched her heavily on one shoulder. She woke, feeling grumpy, with an unseen prodding and nudging against her. The air in the room thickened like gelatin, pushed in upon her and enveloped her.

''Thomas!'' she cried. ''Are you doing that?''

No answer came. She reached for the bedside lamp and flipped on the switch: it made a dull, discordant sound and red darkness overwhelmed her.

''Thomas,'' she cried again. ''Quit teasing.''

A thin, reedy sound returned to her from faraway. ''I don't know where I am,'' Thomas answered. ''Emily . . . Emily?''

The tapping against Emily's shoulder grew agitated. Then it seized her sweater and pulled. Emily slid across the bed, through the thick darkness. With frantic hands she reached out to hold the bed post. But the thing that tugged was persistent and toppled her to the floor. She lay on the carpet for a moment, stunned, frightened and angry. Her emotions bubbled and boiled, and the Chalk Man appeared. His white hands moved quickly across the darkness, and she saw that he drew what appeared to be a gargantuan bottle with stubby wings. He touched the outline and it blazed into a line of fire that crackled and spat. For a brief instant Emily thought she could see a thing imprisoned within the fire, an object shaped like its firey-edge. A thing that opened its jaws, growled and snorted and extinguished the flames.

"It can't be real!" she shouted, and as quickly as the Chalk Man had appeared, he began to fade. She reached out to detain him, but he vanished, and she wished he were back. Emily no longer feared him.

She was tugged again. She twisted, kicked and tried to free herself; she dug her heels into the carpet and felt the material beneath her feet grow thick and spongy. Then suddenly she felt no floor beneath her, and her body seemed to elongate, to stretch out into a thin string of her former self. Whatever held her was smooth and metallic and pulled her along at a tremendous speed.

"Let me go!" she screamed as she raced through the reddish darkness.

"It's time to go, Emily," said a soft male voice that sounded vaguely familiar. "Time to go."

CHAPTER SIX

> This Squick is an obstreperous one. He
> shows inadequate respect, and at times I
> think I'd feel better not dealing with him at
> all. But his Nebulon counts are unsur-
> passed—higher even than my own. If our
> race is to survive, his type must lead. But
> he refuses to marry and sire offspring, damn
> him!
>
> —"The Frozen Journal of Jabu"

She was only a filament, a golden thread ten thousand light-years long that trailed across the heavens
and remembered its name. "I am Emily," it whispered within the cells it called Brain, as though it
wished to remind her of something she had long for-
gotten. Sight existed, though her other senses seemed
to have disappeared or gone to sleep. As she floated,
she could see the great star systems move like jewels
across the universe. One of the jewels flared and
died. Fourth of July, she told herself, Fourth of July,
a time for the night sky to explode with beauty, bits
and pieces of fire flashing through the darkness like
a molten snowfall. And what was the Fourth of July?
She couldn't remember.

She drifted thus, lazily, without fear or sorrow.
Memories crept into her thinking part and she
dreamed soft dreams filled with the faces of those
she loved and places she'd been. A particular face
swam in front of her: Thomas. Where was he? On
the surface of her tranquillity a tiny crack appeared,

just enough to alter the pattern of her being. Things clicked into place, opened and closed and revealed themselves.

Above her head the sky was a cool gray dome. Where had the red darkness gone?

She felt something and realized it was the fabric of her clothing against her hand. Only it wasn't her hand. Her hand ought to have been small, almost square. This one was long-fingered and slender. She searched for the rest of herself and discovered that her legs had stretched and her feet were larger.

Disoriented, she raised herself to a seated position and saw that she rested upon grass. Ordinary, every-day, sweet-smelling grass that stretched outward in a never ending carpet and finally disappeared beneath the edge of a high concrete wall. Nothing marred this expanse of grass except a dark shape sprawled a few meters away. She thought she might be in a park, but noted an absence of swings or trees or flowers.

Emily stood, somewhat shaky, and walked to the edge of the wall to see what lay beyond. Its height obstructed her view, but there was a planter box filled with dirt beside it, and she used this to climb upward. On the other side of the wall there was nothing she could immediately identify, but for a few moments she thought about her geometry class. The scene before her was all planes and angles and vertical and horizontal lines. She focused, but it didn't hold and she had to remember what she'd seen. Buildings, lots of them, a sensation of altitude . . . rooftops visible. Tall, modern structures in the distance, and nearby more buildings—squat, ugly, gray, separated by narrow alleyways filled with refuse.

I'm on top of a building, she thought, and dismissed the idea at once as impossible.

The shape on the grass stirred and groaned, rolled over and faced her.

"Thomas," Emily mumbled. She ran on unfamiliar legs toward an unfamiliar Thomas, an older Thomas.

He gazed at her, and after a blur before her eyes he was as he had been before—green eyes, brown hair, tall and slightly chubby. She looked down at her own body and saw that it was as it always had been—a slender torso attached to short, slim legs. Emily sighed with relief.

Her brother stared at her with widened eyes. "Where are we?"

"I don't know. Outside somewhere." Her answer sounded feeble, and she tried once more. "Looks like a park."

Thomas shook his head as though he wished to dislodge something clinging to his scalp. He flailed his arms about and tried to explain his dream. "I flew through the sky . . . past the stars."

Emily hugged her body to keep from shivering. "I did, too!" she exclaimed. "And the Chalk Man came for an instant. I think he tried to save us from . . . this, whatever it is."

"You really think so?"

"I'm sure of it. This time he was a friend." She sucked in her breath. "It's funny, like I was on the edge of communicating with him. Closer than ever. If Victoria ever heard me say this . . ."

Thomas's forehead creased in a frown, and he shook his round, baby face from side to side. "I always thought you made the Chalk Man happen," he said. "Not on purpose, but because you needed him. I don't know exactly why. What if . . ." He cleared his throat. "What if our minds did this one together, kind of reinforced each other and transported us somewhere, like right here?"

"You always make me feel better about things. Even when I don't understand what you're talking about."

She tried to review the events of her dream, seeking a point where it broke off, where this cold, hard reality came into being. She needed to grasp some sense in their predicament. Emily wished her grandparents, with all their wisdom, were here to help.

Thomas hugged his knees close to his chest and rocked back and forth.

It was a language of fear that he spoke with his body, Emily sensed, though he didn't speak it. She and her brother possessed a kinship that went beyond an ordinary brother-sister relationship. They communicated their needs to each other in effortless ways. Since the day Thomas was born, Emily had felt a particular affinity for him, as though he held a part of her she could never share with another human. They had never discussed their relationship; there seemed no reason to do so. It existed, and that was sufficient.

A motherly streak arose in Emily, and she wanted to comfort her brother. But she knew he would resent such behavior, for while younger, he was almost an inch taller than she and professed a fear of nothing . . . usually. After all, it was she—Emily—who still worried about monsters in her closet and Thomas who chased them from her mind.

Emily studied her brother's worried expression. She didn't know how to help him.

"This is odd-to-the-nth," Thomas said.

She agreed. Unusual events occurred in the world on a daily basis, Emily knew. Television and grocery-store tabloids told the tales. Like the one about the man who disappeared in a flash of lightning. One moment he was alive and talking, and the next he was engulfed in a fireball. Photographers took pictures and the photos revealed only a smudge of black on the ground where the man had stood. Where had he gone? To a place like this?

Fragments of Emily's dream lingered at the back

of her thoughts, but made no sense. A great longing engulfed her and hung heavily upon her spirit. All inner joy seemed to have fled, replaced by an unfillable emptiness. She felt . . . what? Older. Unquestionably so, in a flood of sensations. She held out her hands and turned them this way and that, as though they held the secret to everything. She ran them across the grass and felt its coarse texture. It wasn't real grass after all, but an artificial variety made to look and smell authentic. Yards of artificial grass.

"Fake grass," she said, and she saw that it extended in every direction, up to the edge of a high cement wall that went all around.

An object sped toward them across the grassy plain, a rectangular box suspended a short distance off the ground. As it drew closer, Emily made out decorations along its sides: stars and moons and complicated designs that wound and twisted and appeared to be not only part of the box but part of the air that surrounded it, one melding with the other.

The box came to an abrupt stop a few meters away and settled softly upon the ground. It was large, much taller than Emily, and for a long time it sat there without movement or noise. It was an intimidating presence, and she found the wavy designs bore a dim resemblance to eyes and mouths and teeth.

Then tendrils crept a short distance from the surface of the box, snaked around and retreated quickly, rearranging themselves once more into designs—different designs than before.

Thomas pointed. "Look what it's doing."

The box lid lifted in a quick, jerking motion. A creature came up, with a smiling goat face and a tall fur hat that writhed like a living thing. The goat face bobbed from side to side, and a pink tongue lolled from its mouth.

"Jack-in-the-box," Thomas said, and his face glowed with interest.

"More like a monster-in-the-box," observed Emily, fascinated and frightened at the same time.

The creature held its smile and doffed its hat, then zipped away its face and became Mr. Squick.

Thomas, mouth agape, asked, "How did you do that?"

"Do what?"

"The goat face."

"Endomine is playing tricks on your mind, child. How do you feel? Nice sleep? Endomine is a great tranquilizer."

"What do you mean?" Emily demanded.

"I drugged you. Had to, you see. You slept here all night."

Squick shrugged. "Didn't hurt you, did it?"

"I saw a goat face, too," Emily said. "How is that possible?"

"An unusual effect of the drug," Squick said.

"Where are we?" Thomas asked. "And what's that funny-looking box you're in?"

"Where are you?" Mr. Squick chuckled. "Why, you're here, of course. I came in this carrier"—he pointed to the box—"in order to entertain you. One of the qualities I understand about children is their sense of humor. Humor: It's more than a quality, it seems almost a need. I've tried to accommodate that need. But apparently it's wasted effort." He shook his head. "Can't change the past, but can change the future. Come along with me now." He gestured toward the carrier. "Come on. Come on."

"We're not getting in that thing," Emily said, but she was unsure of her brother's feelings. He seemed deeply interested in the vehicle.

To Emily this plain of false grass might not be home, but it had become familiar and in a peculiar way comforting. It was, she believed, a path home, a rope that held her in place. Nonna or Panona or their father might find the clues that led here, might rescue them.

Nonna's words came back, from a hike they'd been on: *"If you're lost in the woods, remain in one place and await rescue."* In Emily's fertile imagination the blades of artificial grass became a great forest of trees.

She heard a noise, an indeterminate, hostile sound, and Squick's mouth became a ridge of anger. His body hunched over, twitched in an alarming manner, and seemed to expand taller and wider until he loomed over them like a great, furious cloud. Fright squeezed Emily, almost made her whimper. But she made no sound. She watched his eyes blink furiously, and was sure she could hear that strange little grating sound she had heard before.

"Get in the damned box," Squick ordered. "I've had enough of this game."

Robot arms reached out from the box, grasped the children tightly in rubber grippers and stuffed them into the warm, dark box interior.

Squick's voice, heavy with anger, crackled through the darkness. "Get this through your brains. Here you'll do things exactly as I say." The voice softened. "If you cooperate, it won't be so bad."

Emily lay beside her brother at the bottom of the box on something that had the texture of cool glass to her finger touch, though to the rest of her body it felt soft and yielding and warm. She couldn't arrange the sensations logically in her mind, but they persisted nonetheless.

Overhead, Squick sat on a small platform and stared straight ahead, grim-jawed. He breathed loudly several times, a wheezing, and called down to them, "Here we go."

There was a faint rumble of sound and then nothing. No vibration or jiggling or clattering or any impression of movement.

"Are we moving?" Emily asked Thomas. "I can't feel anything."

"I don't know."

"I hear his eyeballs when they move. Can you hear them?"

"Heck no." And Thomas's face took on a peculiar, disbelieving expression reminiscent of Victoria's.

Squick's malevolent laughter ricocheted against the walls of the box. Then, as though he'd experienced a change of heart, he looked down upon the helpless children, smiled benevolently and said, "I want you to consider yourselves my invited guests, to be cherished and treated politely. Sorry if I frightened you back there. I'm a little tired, and my tolerance for children gets low at times. Just doing my job like always, day in and day out."

An exit door opened on the vehicle's side, and Emily felt herself propelled outside by rubber grippers onto a ramp that dropped her to the artificial grass. Thomas came close behind, the same way.

Emily's legs no longer seemed like regular legs, but more the way she imagined a doll's might feel, made of plastic or fabric and useless for locomotion. She took a few tentative steps. Artificial grass still lay beneath her feet, but now a number of live plants in boxes and pots were apparent nearby that she hadn't seen before, and a small, shedlike structure stood in their midst.

"Come, little one," said Squick. He seized her hand and squeezed it until she almost cried out. "I've things to show the two of you." He pulled her toward the structure, which had a peaked roof and two swinging doors.

With his other hand he held Thomas, and they bumped through the swinging doors into the interior

of the shed, a small, bare room. Squick touched
something on his belt, and the wall before them
opened like a mouth. "Slide into the mole tube,"
Squick commanded. "Down we go!"

And he leaped onto a wide, dark slide, still holding onto the children. The slide was slick and smooth
under Emily's bottom, and she sped into darkness.
Around and around they spiraled, traveling steeply
downward. Emily felt warm, clammy air against her
face.

A terrible sense of fear and foreboding came over
her, and she wished she hadn't been forced to take
this ride. *Mole tube?* she thought. *What is a mole
tube?*

"Ooh!" Thomas squealed. "This is fun!"

"Coming up to a landing," Squick said presently.
"Stay on your feet!"

Emily's feet hit the floor before she could think,
and though she stumbled, Squick kept her from falling over. She couldn't see anything.

"Now walk," Squick commanded. "Onto the
ramp."

The ramp went down steeply but not as much as
the slide, and around and around they walked. Emily
became afraid of bumping into something and pulled
back. She groped ahead and to the side with her free
hand, touched nothing. It was pitch black in the tunnel, and Emily could no longer see the man who
held her hand. Nor could she see Thomas.

"Quit lagging," Squick said.

"But it's dark," Emily protested. "I can't see."

"I can see enough for all of us."

"Do you see with magic?" Thomas asked, and
he sounded not in the least afraid. The question surprised Emily, for Thomas had a scientific mind, she
thought, and he didn't believe in magic.

"As you wish" came the cryptic response.

Emily was jerked forward, with such strength that

her arm ached. She scurried to keep up, but the fear
of running into something had not disappeared.

She heard the shuffling of their shoes on a hard,
smooth surface and identified Thomas's steps—a
rapid, echoing patter—then Squick's less frequent but
heavier sounds, and finally her own, a patter lighter
than Thomas's. Were they on concrete, or maybe
hard-packed dirt? She couldn't tell, couldn't recall
any details of the surface from the tunnel entrance.

Squick breathed heavily at her side, and she heard
the clicking and grating of his eyeballs. Might he be
a robot, one that could see in the dark? Such strange
red eyes. But his hand felt warm and human, a little
moist. Or was that perspiration from her own palm?

For an instant Emily thought she heard a whistle
tone singing through the air, high and clear. She
couldn't pick out the sounds of Squick anymore, only
the pattering steps of Thomas and herself in the
darkness.

Malcolm Squick shivered as he recovered from
the tugs and pulls of disunion. He was in two places
at once, via a technology Gweens could never du-
plicate or begin to understand. *Poor, disadvantaged
Gweens!* This Inventing Corps technology, associated with amoeba-cams and stealth mass-shifting
methods, enabled him to divide the tangible spectra
of his body into two sensory realms—leaving at least
one of his five bodily senses in each realm.

This time he left only his sensation of touch in the
tunnels with the children, and though he could not
see, hear or smell them (and could not taste them
had he wanted to), he felt their hands gripped in
each of his own.

He set this division into motion with a precise
whistle tone, one limited to the Ch'Var auditory
range. Squick could activate the Divider from anywhere inside or outside the branch office structure,

without limitation of range, and as with other Ch'Var technology, he didn't concern himself much with its workings. He knew only that it was a mechanism built into the building, originally designed to aid fieldmen in escaping from Gween authorities as necessary. It included an automatic system that warned a fieldman of approaching police, wherever the fieldman happened to be.

If not overridden by a fieldman's conscious effort, the Divider split a fieldman "four and one," leaving only his sense of smell behind while catapulting the body, brain and other four senses to the nearest safe location. The body and brain always went with the majority of senses—with that grouping of at least three senses. Those senses remaining behind, though without body or brain nearby, functioned nonetheless, transmitting sensual data from the original location to the new one.

The system had never failed.

In this disunion Squick had split himself by conscious effort, and the particular whistle tone he selected specified the division of his senses, body and brain. So, while guiding the children through the entrance tunnel, he was simultaneously in a tiny, windowless room deep beneath the surface, ready to ship his embidium orders to the Director. A yellow panel dominating the wall opposite the door would open at the appointed time.

Squick stared at a tray of embidium vials that held purple liquid—those extractions he'd made in recent days. He zeroed in on Thomas Harvey's vial, identifiable by its vial number, and saw the familiar stringy red glow of the Nebulon-encased embidium.

He considered withholding Thomas's embidium, but Jabu knew of the extraction from the transmission to headquarters. Jabu couldn't know he had the children, however, for they'd been kidnapped after the transmission of the Seven Sacred Questions, with answers.

Squick wondered if he should warn the Director this embidium was different, or that it might be different. Or should he just ship it? It would be interesting to see if the boy's embidium, this unusual extraction, could be implanted, therapeutically inserted to give a recipient happy childhood memories. If it didn't take, Jabu wouldn't necessarily say anything. Rejections occurred occasionally for unknown reasons.

To hell with warning him. The boy's fluid clouded when I tested it, so I've done my job, and now it's up to Jabu to follow his own damn steps.

Squick had no knowledge of the implant procedure, only that certain careful steps had to be followed by the Director.

But this embidium might he unlike any Jabu had ever handled; it certainly was a first for Squick.

He felt a child's hand trying to pull away—Emily's—and he gripped it harder.

He knew he should say something to the Director about this extraordinary extraction, that he should speak up before the shipment was made. But something told Squick to keep his silence. He'd taken the Harvey children on impulse, out the side door of their home into his chameleo-van and away. It hadn't been thought out, wasn't logical. Did another force drive him to take the children with him in violation of procedures? He couldn't be certain. But now these children were entirely within his control.

A shudder passed through Squick.

He tried to convince himself his preoccupation with these children wasn't the loathsome, unspeakable type he feared so much. This seemed to emanate from some other driving force, a powerful, more compelling urge than any he had ever known. Something akin to the Nebulons, he thought, and on a vast scale. This urging would not be denied. It did not tickle him or nag him. It demanded his full attention.

In secrecy he would attempt another extraction from the boy, this potential goose with golden eggs. An unlimited supply of embidiums would be interesting, and if Squick controlled the source . . .

I'll have to hide these children somewhere, he thought. *Jabu could spot-check me at any moment, and the risk of that seems higher with what I'm sending him now.*

The yellow wall panel slid open, revealing a small red cage.

Squick released Thomas's hand, and in a blur of hand speed the fieldman lifted the cage top, set his tray of vials inside and reclosed the cage. When his hand was clear, the yellow panel slid shut. Once again he grasped Thomas's hand. Squick didn't know how the vial shipment system worked, only that it did. Director Jabu's headquarters were linked to this and all other field buildings in a mysterious way, one of the secrets that only the Director and his prized Inventing Corps knew.

Certainly Mother Ch'Var had never had anything like this.

Squick wondered what the alpha-mother would want him to do in this circumstance, and he tried to tell himself he wasn't behaving selfishly, that the Harvey information was safest with him.

But the troubled fieldman could not convince himself, and from all angles of thought he realized more than ever that he wanted to be Director, that this factor would have to be entered into the complicated equation of his actions.

CHAPTER SEVEN

"Sometimes it matters most not what is
there, but what might be there."
　　　　　　　—Emily to her brother
　　　　　　　in a dream

Emily gave up trying to pull her hand away. The grip
was too strong, and it disturbed her that she hadn't
heard a peep from Squick for several minutes. She
squinted, shifted her parallax in increasing light and
saw Squick seem to appear from midair, taking shape
from a thickening mist of human form.

An impossibility. A trick of lights or from the
drugs, she decided.

In the back of Emily's mind she thought she heard
a high, clear whistle tone like the earlier one, faint
and brief in duration.

"Kidnapper!" Emily shouted.

"A harsh word," answered Squick. "I look on
your circumstance in a different light. You are guests
about to take a tour of facilities. Think of this occasion as a special treat, one we usually don't extend
to clients."

Emily's voice rose. "Treat? Mistreat is more like
it. My dad has the police after you, and you'll go to
jail forever! They're looking for us now, and you'd
better let us go!"

The crescendo of her voice silenced her. What
good did it do to shout? Squick was large, powerful
and in total control. And while her father searched

85

for her, what would this stranger do to them? Who was Squick—or rather, what was he? With his personality shifts, he might be a psychopath, without conscience. A shudder of fear shook her, and she decided to behave more cooperatively, at least until she could discover a way to escape.

Light from ahead filtered into the tunnel way, enabling her to see Squick and her brother more clearly.

Squick released his grip on Thomas, and the boy increased his pace, moving by himself several meters ahead. Emily could tell by the way Thomas's head cocked to one side and the manner in which he slapped his right hand against his leg that he was totally and blindly fascinated by this place.

"What's up ahead?" Thomas asked.

"You mean down ahead?" Squick retorted with a chuckle.

"Yes!" There was no animosity in the boy's tone, only playfulness, and Emily wished he could be more perceptive. He didn't seem cognizant of any danger, but Emily sensed otherwise.

Why has this man taken us?

Squick's voice intruded upon her thoughts, and he spoke low enough that Thomas didn't hear. "I don't have to let you go, as you put it. While I was in your home, after administering the drugs I left a little message on your answering machine that turns your threats into . . . nothing."

She turned her head and glared.

They entered a narrow, brilliantly illuminated room, and a door that Emily hadn't noticed snapped shut behind them. The light in the room metamorphosed from white to a wild array of sparking colors, creating the illusion they were in the midst of a noiseless fireworks explosion.

"We're in a stealth-lock," Squick said, "becoming invisible to anyone . . . outside."

Emily experienced a pleasant tingling, and before

she could phrase a question the room opened to a wide, brightly lit chamber filled with party supplies arranged in neat rows on storage racks. Two pyramid-shaped robots worked the aisles, and a short, jowly man in a shiny yellow onesuit seemed to be supervising them while they transferred objects back and forth. Emily recognized some of the same articles she had seen in Squick's briefcase—party hats, tablecloths, food sample packets . . .

Thomas ran to one of the racks, examined a plastic bag of toy cars.

"You're wondering about the answering machine," Squick said to Emily. "Isn't that right, little one?" He smirked and released her hand.

She moved a short distance away, afraid to go farther or to call out for her brother.

"Want to know the message I left?" Squick asked. "I altered my voice to sound like your father's— we're trained to do that. I copied his voice from the master tape and told your housekeeper that Victoria and I—your father, that is—picked you kids up and took you to San Margarita." He grinned. "Nobody's gonna miss you for days."

Emily shook her head as she watched Thomas peer into the sealed cello bag of toy cars. Such intense interest in his eyes, and she realized her brother's curiosity kept him from fear. At least for the moment. She wanted to get to him, to talk with him.

"Dad will call," Emily said, "and he'll get through to Mrs. Belfer."

"Maybe not. Victoria will keep your old man busy, count on that."

Emily choked back a sob.

Squick pointed to a stairway just to Emily's left. "Down the stairs," he ordered. "Thomas! Over here!"

Thomas replaced the cello bag on the shelf and

ran to join his sister and Squick. "Neat-o stuff!" the
boy said.

"One of our warehouse areas," Squick said, slid-
ing toward the doorway. "We have warehouses all
over the world, full of lots of things. We manufac-
ture toys and tanks and guns and dolls and drugs
and, well, you name something and we handle it."

"I thought you were a caterer," Emily said.

"That too," Squick said. "It's a diversified operation. The man in the yellow onesuit is my assistant, Peenchay. Not very bright, but a hard worker.
That's all we can count on these days, isn't it, labor
problems being what they are?" When the children
didn't respond, he added, "Say, you like that bag of
cars, Tom-Tom? It's yours."

"Yay!" Thomas retrieved the bag of cars.

Metal clanged as they descended the stairs, playing ugly music in Emily's ears. For a while she
counted the number of flights: two, three, four, five
. . . they kept going. The air in this passageway was
filled with an assortment of odors, and Emily identified some: paint and glue and wet paper. What was
this place? She resisted voicing the question, afraid
she would irritate Squick. He might not be truthful
anyway.

At the bottom of the steps they reached a door
with a sign on it that made no sense to Emily: "NEB-
ULON POWER!"

"What's that mean?" asked inquisitive Thomas.

"Exactly what it says," Squick answered. He
opened the door and led them into a golden room.
Sparkling bric-a-brac cluttered long tables, dripped
from the walls, lay on the floors. Golden ribbons,
chains, loops and bows and spools of metal lace, all
glitter and flash.

"It's beautiful," whispered Emily, and instantly
hated herself for saying anything pleasant to Squick.

"Minor part of our operation," Squick replied.

"We construct party favors on this floor, and this is the gold room. Come along, more to see. You wait here, Tom-Tom. Emily will appreciate the next room more than you."

"We'd like to stay together," Emily said, but her voice was small and seemed to go unnoticed.

Thomas, Emily observed, was busy inspecting a golden train set and didn't notice when Squick ushered her forcibly from the room.

"Thomas," she squeaked, and was immediately silenced by a sharp twist Squick gave her arm.

"No complaints," Squick warned in a low voice. "Let's not upset your brother. Say something nice to Tom-Tom, Emily."

"Stay here, Thomas," Emily said. "I'll be back in a little while."

"Such a good girl," Squick whispered, a rasp. He hustled her out and down a long, barren corridor lined with doors, pushed one open and they entered darkness.

"This is the place," Squick said in a flat, cold voice.

"Where are we?" Emily asked.

"Not quite the lowest level, but what do you care?"

The game he had played in Thomas's presence ceased, all pretense of joviality vanished, and Emily was left alone with a man who had the freedom to do whatever he wished with her in an unlit room. What would he do? She remembered Mrs. Belfer's warnings about strange men in strange places who did strange things. She thought about school and how the eighth grade girls discussed s-e-x with one another and giggled over its knowns and unknowns. Some of the more knowledgeable girls, the ones who watched soap operas and read romance novels and had dates, were more specific about the details.

Emily had but one experience, during the previous

summer vacation. It was a story she'd never related to any of the other girls, fearing their derision. She'd always had trouble forming friendships because of her shyness. She was smaller than the other girls in her class, too, and this bothered her.

Her experience, if she could call it that, concerned an older boy who had taken her sailing. He was the son of a bank executive and his parents belonged to the tennis club, so Victoria gave immediate permission for the date. At the first opportunity when they were on the water, the boy tried to pull Emily's blouse off. She kicked him hard in the groin, dove overboard and swam to shore. Not much chance for that sort of escape now, and she had Thomas to worry about as well.

Squick turned on the light. "Welcome to our game room."

The room was filled with gadgets, games and dolls. A puppet theater dominated one corner, with red velvet curtains across a gilt-edged stage. Two exquisitely fabricated puppets dangled from the curtain rod. Their tiny wooden hands clung to the strings that held them, each finger a perfect replica of a human's.

One of the puppets, with glitter-green eyes, looked a bit like Thomas.

"Have fun," Squick said. "I'll be back for you." He stepped through the door, closed it.

Emily heard the click of a lock.

CHAPTER EIGHT

> I wonder what it's like undergoing an embidium extraction. Has it ever been attempted on a Ch'Var?
>
>> —From an anonymous letter to the Director

It was a golden train, an engine and five passenger cars, on a golden track in a golden room, and Squick paused momentarily in the doorway to watch the boy roll the train back and forth.

The boy looked up and smiled quizzically.

"Hello, Tom-Tom," Squick said.

"It doesn't have a motor. I looked."

"That doesn't mean one isn't there." Squick approached, sizing up his prey, this remarkable child. The Harvey boy seemed alert and unchanged despite the extraction, and he had a trusting openness about him. It almost seemed too easy, as if a trap had been set for Squick.

But what sort of trap could this be? From children? Squick recalled his childhood ethics classes and a folktale, "Rescue of the Gweens," about an evil Ch'Var who preyed upon Gweenchildren and abused them sexually. In the story Lordmother intervened, and the Ch'Var, having lost face, committed ritual shittah.

Squick placed a hand on the boy's shoulder, felt the delicate child bones beneath the fabric of Thomas's shirt. Bones fragile enough to snap.

Thomas pulled away and lowered his face to the level of the train's engine car, peering through openings in the side of the toy. He lifted it from the track, unhitched the coupling that held it to the string of cars and let the cars back down on the track.

"There's no motor in there!" Thomas insisted.

"I didn't say where it was."

"You're teasing!"

"Do you like this game?"

"Where's the motor? In one of the other cars?"

"Look in the mirror."

"What mirror? What do you mean? Oh, you mean I'm . . . ?"

Squick nodded. "You're the motor, whenever you push it. The thing's made of gold. Every item in this room is, with varying alloys. Maybe a golden engine wasn't practical."

Gold, gold, Squick thought. *Are you the goose with golden eggs? Lay me another embidium, goose!*

In one of Squick's hands appeared an array of nearly flat candy bars in varying fruit and chocolate flavors, held like playing cards. "Pick a candy, any candy," he said.

Thomas held back, then grabbed a chocolate bar.

"Your reward for winning the engine game." In a blink the remaining candy bars were gone.

Thomas tore the wrapper from his treat, and with his teeth he pulled away a large hunk of chocolate taffy. He began chewing it. The gooey candy left a pattern of brown around the edge of his lips, a clown design that enlarged his mouth.

"Would you like to play more games?" Squick asked.

The Harvey boy nodded, and Squick saw he was laboring to chew the candy.

"Now we'll play the breakfast game, and that's why I gave you candy first. Guest children get to have candy with every meal."

Thomas swallowed a lump of candy and said, "I don't know how to play the breakfast game."

"Oh but you do, only I'm going to show you a different version, one for kids."

Squick led the way down a corridor lined with emerald green walls. Light glowed from behind the walls and cast patterns of green across the boy's face and T-shirt. They passed an alcove lined in silver, from which an eyeless face stared. The eyes had been gouged away hideously, and the sockets dripped blood.

The boy suppressed a scream.

"Just a party display," Squick said. "Some kids like horror fetes, and they get pretty elaborate. Look, there's another!"

On their left through a large window of glass, a pond became visible, bobbing with floating bloody heads. They were eyeless and gory like the head in the alcove, but the mouths of these heads moved, as though talking to one another. No sounds reached the corridor.

"Yuk!" Thomas said, pausing with Squick to gaze at the display. Thomas finished his candy bar, balled up the wrapper and held onto it.

"You can toss the wrapper. Just sling it. Littering is the law here, young man."

Thomas looked surprised, but let the wrapper fall.

"No social rules here whatsoever, so litter to your heart's content. Would you like a can of spray paint to deface something?"

"But the hallway's clean except for my wrapper. And I don't see any graffiti."

"New rules."

"Oh."

"Things are always changing. That's important to understand."

They reached the lunch room, and once inside with the boy, Squick locked the door surreptitiously.

He motioned his unwitting captive toward a long table, and as Thomas took a seat on one of the benches, the tabletop budded open before him, producing a white linen tablecloth and napkin, a bone china cereal bowl and plate, a silver place setting, and a crystal juice glass.

Two robot arms with giant hands descended from the ceiling. One hand held a yellow metal basket, and the hand of the other arm dipped into the basket, producing sweet rolls, doughnuts, an array of little cereal boxes, cans of juice, and plates with steaming eggs sunny-side up, pancakes, sausages, and assorted melons. Crystal pitchers of sugar, maple and fruit syrups, cream, and milk completed the fare. A pleasant mixture of odors filled the air.

"Neat-o," Thomas exclaimed, his eyes wide. "I'm hungry."

The mechanical arm and basket disappeared into the ceiling.

"No social rules?" Thomas asked while he held a doughnut and gazed impishly at Squick.

"None whatsoever."

Thomas hurled the doughnut across the room, grabbed another and stuffed it in his mouth and smashed his fist down upon the sweet rolls. He filled his bowl with cereal and cream and too much sugar, slurped several spoonfuls, burped gigantically, and wiped his face on the tablecloth.

"That's all?" Squick asked.

"Not quite." Thomas stood up and yanked the tablecloth, pulling everything to the floor. China, crystal and food crashed in a great, inundating noise.

"Goodness!" Squick exclaimed, stepping quickly to avoid a stream of berry syrup that drooled across the floor. "You are a bad little boy!"

Thomas burped again, followed by a rumble of flatulence. "What's next?"

"I see you're getting warmed up."

The robot arms reemerged from the ceiling, this time with cleaning supplies. The arms stretched and moved in precise, methodical circles as they tidied away the mess. One arm sprayed Thomas's face, and the other wiped it with a towel. Dishes and garbage were removed, tables and benches were lifted into ceiling compartments. Presently the room was entirely barren of furnishings.

Squick heard a subsonic signal and opened the door. Peenchay stood there, bowing slightly with his tiny ochre-red eyes lowered. Something gray and glistening hung from his lower lip, a piece of Gweenbrain from Peenchay's last meal. His tongue lashed out, pulled the fragment in and he swallowed.

Like a damned frog, Squick thought. *Or a toad.* Indeed, the Inferior reminded him in body structure of such an amphibian. Squick detected an odor of decaying meat.

"You have an amoeba-cam?" Squick asked. *What a curious diet for the penultimate fool,* he thought. *You'd think some of that Gween gray matter would seep in.*

"Here, sir." Peenchay extended one open palm containing a blue-green device in the shape of a tiny round pill.

Squick plucked it from the proffered palm and snapped, "Change your clothes and bathe."

"Now?"

"Immediately, if not sooner!"

When Peenchay was gone, Squick relocked the door and returned to the boy. Holding up the amoeba-cam, Squick asked, "Can you see this?"

"Your hand?"

"I'm holding something."

"Another game?"

Squick detected a modicum of fear in the boy's eyes, and the fieldman trembled, a familiar sensation. Soon Nebulons would flow from his body into the boy's . . .

"No games." Squick flipped the amoeba-cam in the air, and it buzzed into flight, a pale red glow to him. "You still see nothing?"

"Am I . . . supposed to imagine? You threw something?"

"No games, I said."

"I hear buzzing, like a fly."

"Aha! Just like before, when I was in your house?"

Thomas nodded. "Invisible insects?"

"Bugs of a sort" came the response, and Squick felt his mouth shape into a sardonic smile. But it didn't hold. "Only Ch'Vars can hear their sound."

"Only what? Can we get back to the games? Please, Mr. Squick?" More fear than before in the eyes, and in the boy's tone of voice.

"You are not Ch'Var. I see that in your eyes." But Squick wondered if the Nebulon count in this boy might be so low that the red of Nebulons didn't show in his irises. This fieldman had never heard of or encountered a Ch'Var with such an extreme condition, but he thought it possible. According to stories long told among his people, the irises of ancient Ch'Vars were ruby red. Then over millenia, a fading, a washing away.

Ruby eyes! What a sight they must have been!

"What are you talking about? What's a Ch'Var?"

Squick glowered at the boy and said, "And your sister claims she hears the grating of my eyeballs. Even Ch'Vars do not hear that, if such a sound exists. Yet in all ways our senses are superior to Gween senses."

"I don't know what you—"

"Shut up! You don't need to understand! Strange children. Come here, strange one."

The boy's chin quivered and he didn't obey. He appeared ready to cry.

"Here! Now!"

Thomas shuffled over, made whimpering sounds.

Squick touched the tear ducts of his own eyes, felt the icy flow of Nebulons, and within moments the ancient, memory-seeking organisms entered the boy's body through Thomas's eyes to his brain.

The boy slumped to the floor, and a scream issued from him, a high trill that sent Squick backward several steps.

The child was in a prenatal position, not uncommon in extraction cases, but the muscles of his throat convulsed, discharging volleys of shuddering screams into the room. The terrible sounds filled Squick's body, blocked thought, and he ran back to the door, fumbled with the lock mechanism and thrust the door open.

When he was in the corridor with the door closed, Squick still heard the screams, and still his body was invaded with sound, unabated in intensity.

He touched a signal button on the underside of his belt, and Peenchay came, wearing a vapid expression.

"Sir?"

"Shut him up," Squick yelled.

A horrible smile consumed the Inferior's features.

"Not that way," Squick snapped. "Drug this one. Keep him alive, but get him away from me! The noise is unbearable! Put him in a basement room where I won't hear him. Don't just stand there, idiot. Do as I say. And don't harm the boy. Hear me?"

Peenchay's eyes flashed in momentary anger, and Squick wondered: *Would you eat my brains given the opportunity? I think you might, idiot Inferior.*

Frozen fear permeated Squick's bones. He shuddered, envisioning Peenchay in a murderous frenzy, tearing into the brains of Gweenchildren, ripping out the gray, pink, bloody matter within their skulls and stuffing it into his mouth.

And one of Peenchay's ghoulish descriptions came back, the way he said he tasted sweetness just before he filled his mouth in his abhorrent way—sweetness in his saliva before the taste of Gweenmeat—gushing saliva. Gushing, stinking saliva. And the flavor of the meat, he said, matched the saliva.

Now Peenchay took on the bowed expression of a subordinate sorry for an infraction. Squick reminded himself once again of the assistant's great loyalty to him, and the feelings of uneasiness began to subside.

Peenchay carried the boy away, and a semblance of peace returned to Squick's body. It wasn't the same as before, however. He doubted he could ever forget the screaming of Thomas Harvey. Gweenchildren had screamed occasionally during extractions, and especially when Peenchay got to them, but never anything like this.

I'll let the boy rest and try again later. An extraction only.

He thought of the Harvey girl, of her embidium. *Perhaps I'll extract from her first . . .*

Squick went to his private apartment two levels up, intending to rest and clear his thoughts for determination of the best course of action. In the quiet of his room, in a caressing darkness that sank around and upon him, Squick felt frigid, flowing Nebulons in his eyes and just behind the eyes, Nebulons that danced against and through the implanted Gween-boy embidium he carried in his brain.

He'd been happy with the implant at first—the melding of Gween and Ch'Var had been exceptionally smooth—and life had been better then. But lately, more and more over the years, he realized he felt fragmented and confused. His body and mind were unclear battlegrounds, with warring parties pulling at him . . . and a suggestion of programming, of something he didn't wish to do. And the warring parties, the forces on these hazy, blended fields of combat, were as fuzzy as the battlegrounds themselves. Mental, physical and spiritual powers washed together with ancient tradition, tumbling and flowing in a wet glue of Nebulons.

The face of the boy within flashed: wild hair and jagged, uneven teeth. He was ferocious, riding a long, lean Ch'Var hound.

It wasn't merely a matter of Ch'Var against Gween, of his Ch'Var body rejecting the embidium implant, though he was beginning to surmise that this may have been part of it. Implant rejections were rare, and if they occurred they usually occurred soon after the procedure, within months. But some rejections took longer, many years.

Gradually the frigid flow of Nebulons coursing through Squick's body became warm, a soothing temperature, and he felt anesthetized.

Thomas lay in moisture, warm like the fluid of his mother's womb. Eyeless heads floated in that fluid, and the boy was one. His mouth moved but made no sound, and he tasted blood from his gouged-away eyes.

It was reddish dark in the womb, the redness of blood, and his body formed into a red-irised eye, a single eye about to be born. The taste of blood intensified, and in a torrent he drank of his own fluids, to his fill and beyond. He emerged from the womb, and the eye that was Thomas fled across a desert expanse, into the teeth of poisonous sands borne on a storm wind, sands that were lethal pellets penetrating the cells and tissues of his existence.

He spiraled through the Earth like a stone from the sky, dropping away from the desert storm. Somewhere children were laughing, and he saw a girl swinging a baseball bat at an object that dangled before her, at an animal, a pig. The pig was alive but constructed of paper and glue, and when the girl hit it the pig split asunder horribly, releasing gory gifts from its innards.

These were not toys or candies or bright baubles. They were snakes and body parts and puddles of slime and eyeballs, all writhing and smelling of sewage. The children gathered them anyway, laughing and squealing with delight, and they ate the stinking things, stuffing them down one another's throats.

He saw Booger, his old friend, if indeed he'd ever been a friend. Booger who liked to smash things. Booger's face leaned close, and he could see the gap between Booger's teeth, with those thick, chapped lips opening and closing like the mouth of a giant, ugly fish.

"Hi ho, Tom-Tom," said Booger. "Come to play? Remember all the fun we used to have? You had the toys and I smashed them. Wow, those were the times. Let's do it again!" And Booger's mouth opened so wide that Thomas could see the flabby pink flap at the rear of his throat.

Thomas was one of the eyeballs scooped up by the children. He entered the black tunnel of Booger's throat and tried to prevent a plunge downward, but with no feet, no hands, and something slimy covering his body, he could only speed through darkness and obscenities to land in a pit of steaming, burning bile. Within his nightmare he blacked out. Or thought he did.

In a vision within a vision he saw an information booth before him with desks and computers on the other side. A single pair of eyes floated before one of the desks, green eyes with a ghost of gray face surrounding, a face so hazy that it could barely be seen. Then he saw another pair of eyes, darker and surrounded by a halo of gray hair. Recognition hit him.

"Panona, Nonna!" he cried to the bodiless faces. "It's me, Thomas. Help me!"

"We give away a free case of orange soda with every purchase," the brown eyes that were his grandmother said.

"The way out is not the same as the way in," said the green ones that were his grandfather.

The sets of eyes, each from their hazes, gazed upon Thomas with great tenderness and sadness.

Beneath the information sign hung another, and it read, "NO QUESTIONS."

CHAPTER NINE

"How curious that Nebulons flow from tear
ducts!"

—A trainee, to Director Jabu
(from the Director's notes)

Mrs. Belfer stood, sullen and uncommunicative, in
the center of the Harveys' living room. Her face was
flushed, red wig askew. Near her, Victoria Harvey
smoked a pink nicotine tube which she inhaled and
exhaled in short, rapid bursts as though she were
short of breath. A long blue and white scarf hung
over one shoulder, and she tugged and smoothed the
scarf nervously, trying to arrange it properly.

"Where are they, Mrs. Belfer?" Dr. Harvey said,
picking up the alcohol stench of the housekeeper
even at the distance he stood from her. "We come
home from our trip and my kids are gone. Where
are they?"

He flipped on a floorlamp, chasing evening shadows.

"I told you," Mrs. Belfer mumbled in a thick
voice. "Your phone message said they was goin' with
you. I don't know nothin' else 'cept they was with
their grandfolk yesterday."

"I never left a message," Dr. Harvey said. "You
didn't check for them last night?"

"Didn't see no reason to, after the message. They
mighta been here, I dunno."

"Stop talking about a message, dammit!"

Mrs. Belfer wrinkled her features into a gargoyle expression, shrugged her shoulders and stumbled out of the room.

"Come back here," Dr. Harvey demanded. When she didn't, he said to his wife, "That woman is fired. She's a liar, a drunken derelict and a lousy house-keeper."

Victoria tugged on his sleeve and said, "But darling, she's explained everything she knows. Don't do anything rash. She's a big help to me."

Dr. Harvey tried to retain his composure, watched through the living room window as a streetlight flickered on.

"Darling?" Victoria said.

He wiped perspiration from his face with a shirt-sleeve, and with measured words said, "Something's terribly wrong here. I'd better call the police, like Mom and Dad suggested."

"This isn't an emergency yet. Nonna and Panona saw them less than twenty-four hours ago."

"Well, I'm damned worried. This is a big city and—"

"I specifically told them to stay home today," Victoria interjected with a tug on her scarf. "They probably went somewhere this morning and lost track of time."

"God, I hope they weren't out last night."

Victoria's voice softened and her quick, nervous gestures smoothed to fluidity. She collected herself into an attractive package: chin out, breasts high, skirt straightened, scarf in place. Her lavender eyes opened wide until they appeared childlike. "Sweet-heart . . . Patrick . . . I know you love Emily, but she does have some serious problems. That's why we send her to a therapist. She's a difficult child. I've tried to get close to her, tried to give her love, but she resents me, pushes me away. She's full of hatred. And her wild imagination . . . invisible bugs

and other things. I think we need to talk about maybe
. . . mmmm, uh, getting her into a facility.''

"What's that supposed to mean?''

"She needs more care than a therapist can supply.
Round-the-clock care, a year or two in a place where
they can watch her and give her the kind of help we
both want her to have.''

"Maybe she doesn't like it here because of your
incompetent parenting, Victoria. I'm tired of hearing
you say she's crazy. I think she's a fine girl, and
she'd be more normal if you let up on her. Maybe
you're the problem, not her.''

The stylish eyebrows arched, like the spines of
cats. "Incompetent parenting? Where are you when
these kids need you? Off in some hospital or talking
about going to operate on Mexican compañeros.
You're needed here.''

"Don't try to dump it on me, you selfish, spoiled . . .''
She stared bullets at him.

"As far as Mexico goes,'' Dr. Harvey said, "all
those people who need me so desperately are going
to have to wait. I can't leave with all this happening.''

"And I suppose that's my fault?'' Angrily she
snuffed her nicotine tube in the oxygen-vac of an
ashtray.

"We're wasting time.'' Dr. Harvey lifted the telephone receiver and pressed the police button.

Victoria was an angry whirl of skirts in the hallway as she moved swiftly toward the kitchen and
back porch. She yanked open the door of Mrs. Belfer's room.

Bottle in hand, Mrs. Belfer lay sprawled across
her bed, eyes closed. The room was cluttered with
dirty dishes and clothes, and her red wig lay on a
lace pillow beside her like an exotic pet that might

suddenly rise on tiny feet to snap and snarl at an intruder.

"What the hell are you up to?" Victoria cried. "What are you trying to do to me? Where are the kids?"

The woman on the bed roused herself to a seated position. "How do I know? What do you care? You got the doctor all to yourse'f now. Ain't that what you wanted? Mr. Rich and all his money, with no one to spend it on or leave it to except poor, sweet Victoria."

Victoria felt the muscles of her mouth tighten. "Look here, you drunken bitch, don't play funny with me. You're only here because I allow it."

"Ha!" screamed Mrs. Belfer. "Don't threaten me, Miss Goodie-Sweet. I hold the gun, not you." She paused, a poignant moment, and her eyes danced wickedly. "What if I was to walk right up to your husband and say, Doc, did you know I used to work for Victoria's folks? Yessirree, I was the cook when they lived in that great big mansion on the hill. Before they lost all their money payin' off their daughter's liability suits and bills. I know all about Miss Goodie-Sweet, the spoiled sorority girl. And I know all about her parties when her folks was gone. Naked boys and girls playin' nasty little games. I got my hands on nice videotapes of those parties. Triple-X stuff."

"Shut up! Shut up!"

"And I'd say, Doc, Miss Goodie-Sweet and her friends wasn't so stuck up in them days. Once in a while they'd even invite a poor kid over for a good time." Mrs. Belfer caught her breath. "Remember, Victoria? The skinny little girl you invited up for a swim? The kid that drowned? And all you naked rich kids standin' around laughin' and makin' a videotape while the kid yelled for help? I got that tape hid real good, Vickie-Sweet. Real good."

Victoria's eyes were dark with rage. "You have a permanent job here, a permanent home thanks to me. All it costs you is silence."

The bottle touched Mrs. Belfer's lips, and she tipped her head back, inhaled deeply and took a long drink. In a moment her gaze returned to level, and the bleary look in her small, blue eyes cleared a little. "Wouldn't that make a good story in the society column? Local doc's wife—"

Victoria's hand shot out and snapped across the side of Mrs. Belfer's cheek. "Keep still about this, or you'll be still for a damned long time. Understand, bitch?"

Mrs. Belfer giggled, lifted her finger in an obscene gesture and fell back upon her bed. As Victoria watched through narrowed eyes, Mrs. Belfer closed her eyes, cradled her bottle and began to snore loudly.

CHAPTER TEN

My brother spoke to me, but without moving his lips. The message was in his eyes,
and I understood it completely.
—*Recollections of Emily Harvey*,
Twenty-second edition

For a while after Squick left her alone, Emily stared
through the semidarkness at the door handle. She
thought she'd heard a lock click when the door closed
behind him, but she comforted herself with the
thought that the mechanism normally made such
sounds, that she wasn't locked in this room at all.
She could turn the handle and leave any time she
wished. But what if it wouldn't open? She wasn't
sure she wanted to find out.

Emily was distracted and fascinated by the contents of the room, particularly by a row of big,
cherubic-faced dolls. Their bland, innocent features
gave her an odd sort of reassurance, a sense that
nothing could go wrong with them around.

But her gaze flickered between the dolls and the
door handle. It was an oversized, round handle,
sculpted to resemble a ball of yellow yarn. A tiny
gray and white kitten with an end of yarn in its teeth
was sculpted on one side of the ball, as if the yarn
were a planet and the kitten an inhabitant.

A chrome machine on her left resembled a soda
fountain unit with a row of flexible white spouts on
its top edge. The mouth of each spout was formed

differently, and from each mouth dribbled small amounts of a substance that looked goopy and reminded her of soft ice cream or cake topping, each dribble a different color. A blue and yellow sign on the unit read, "THE ARTFUL LOOPER," and beneath that Emily found instructions in very small print for making "art loops."

Tentatively she pushed one of the spouts and white, spaghetti-shaped material oozed out and bobbed into the air. According to the instructions, the substance was lighter than air. Emily bent over and read the balance of the written material. With one hand she grabbed the loose end of the artificial spaghetti, looped it around and completed a circle by detaching the other end of the substance from the spout. The goop was only a little sticky to her touch, but adhered to itself nicely and hardened in a few seconds.

She became immersed in creativity, and momentarily this soothed her concerns about Squick and the door handle.

Next she created eyes, a nose and a mouth, all of which she suspended in the center of the oval to form a face. She moved the loops around a little, and they remained where she wanted them, floating in midair. With more effort she made a body, a rumpled white suit, white shoes and white gloves.

"Hello, Chalk Man," she whispered, delighted with the excellence of her work. "Talk to me, Chalk Man. I'm frightened here, and I don't know what to do."

She tried to imagine the Chalk Man's mouth moving, answering her, but no sound came forth. The only movement she detected in her art piece occurred when she moved about and caused air currents to buffet the creature slightly, as a boat might do in the wake of another. She gave the creature a shove and it floated away.

"A stupid game," Emily muttered, and her fears intensified.

The door squeaked behind her, and with that the Chalk Man collapsed to the floor, like a pile of spaghetti without any sauce.

"Oh!" she exclaimed, and for a moment she knelt beside her fallen friend, as if it had been a real, living creature.

A shadow loomed over her, and she looked up into the red-eyed countenance of Mr. Squick.

"I've decided we need to become friends," he said with a thin, ugly smile that Emily found frightening.

"I don't like you."

Squick knelt beside her, and Emily didn't like the way he stared at her, the way his eyes were hard.

"I think," she said, "that you are not a nice person. I want you to let us go home."

"You don't want to be my friend, then?" he asked, wrinkling his face as if in pain.

"You'd better leave me alone."

"Or what?"

"I'll kick you."

Squick laughed, but uneasily. "What I have in mind won't hurt you a bit. There's a little secret thing my people have practiced for thousands of years. Wouldn't you like to know about it?"

"No!" shouted Emily, and she scooted away from him to the other side of her fallen Chalk Man.

"Aren't you going to ask about my people?"

"Where's my brother?"

"Resting." Squick's eyes were a brighter red than usual and moist, his full mouth now a thin, terse line.

Squick trembled and dabbed one of his eyes with a fingertip.

Emily leaped to her feet and darted for the door. She tried to turn the handle, but it wouldn't move.

So she put all her strength into it, and this time something broke off in her hand. When she spread open her fingers, she saw the sculpted kitten, broken free from its world.

A strong hand gripped her shoulder, pulled her backward and Emily screamed. As she went over she saw the row of fat dolls staring down at her with unblinking, uncaring eyes.

Emily lost her vision to a freezing storm that inundated her eyes, drowning her in an ugly ecstasy that did not belong to her. All of her senses succumbed to the storm, and every cell of her body froze into dormancy. She was a block of ice floating in midair—and like the Chalk Man, unable to speak. Then the Chalk Man's words crackled through the air, in Emily's own voice. The ice broke, splitting into particles that rocketed to all parts of the universe.

"Lordmother," called her voice, from thoughts not her own.

She was immersed within the great, pulsing heart of aliens who called themselves Ch'Vars. But they were human, much as she was human, and they walked where she walked, spoke her language, ate her food, and called her Gween. She sensed their thoughts, their pleasures, their pains, and within the depths of this illusion fused with reality, a presence touched her and gave her power.

"Move with me," said the presence, *"and I will help you."*

"I'm beginning to understand," Emily said.

She emerged from the darkness, and her sight returned. Emily lay on her side without movement, peering at Malcolm Squick as he knelt nearby and dipped his finger into a vial of clear liquid. He did not look in her direction.

"I know something," Emily said in a flat, low-pitched voice.

Startled, Squick glanced at her, then looked back at the vial and cursed. "Turn purple, dammit."

"I don't want to turn purple."

"The fluid, not you!"

"Your Nebulons are dead."

"Damn!" Squick hurled the vial across the room, smashing glass and splattering liquid on a wall. "What's gone wrong here?"

Emily continued in the same toneless voice. "I've defeated them."

Squick's cheeks reddened, and deep, angry ridges split his features.

"Your Nebulon count is zero," Emily said.

"You're crazy."

"I know your history," she told him, and she felt herself coming out of a strange dream. Or had it been a dream? The images were slipping away, fading. Still, she understood that Squick was a Ch'Var with an unpleasant black fog that consumed him and concealed a monster beneath the surface. This Ch'Var, like some others, had done terrible things to children, unspeakable things. He invaded their brains, left them to die . . .

I see your filthy soul! she thought, and she wanted to be free of it.

Desperately, Squick went to one eye with a fingertip, then to the other eye. Terror consumed his face.

She reached into her troubled, fading dream and said, "From your Nebulons I know that Gweenchildren disappear, and you are among those responsible. The sleeping sickness explained."

The man was trembling before her.

Emily felt her eyes blazing. "And I know you've tried an extraction on my brother, you bastard. He resisted you, too!"

Squick shot to his feet and backed up, staring at her with eyes that had lost their redness. He fumbled with the door handle, nearly fell into the corridor trying to get away, and slammed the door behind him. The door made its clicking noise again.

Emily opened one hand. The sculpted kitten remained there, and righting it upon her palm, she ran her fingers gently over the tiny gray and white object. Its surface alternated smooth and rough, smooth and rough, smooth and rough . . .

A vast storehouse of racial information had arrayed itself before her, and though it eluded her momentarily she realized with mounting excitement, *I'll never be like I was again. I've changed forever.*

Had Thomas weakened the Nebulons during the extraction attempt on him, enabling her to go a step further? Perhaps, the girl thought, but she sensed more than this. Much more.

And she worried about her brother.

Squick, upset by Emily's bitter words, paced restlessly in his office. Why the hell should he care if a Gweengirl insulted him? But he did care, in a way he didn't understand.

He rummaged about in his desk for the chocolate nut bar he'd placed there earlier under his cash-expenditure book. A small, wild laugh burst from his mouth. *My damned pacifier . . . that's what it is and it isn't here. Did Peenchay get into my stuff?*

He stalked down the hall, through the stealth-lock and out into the Gween world in the downstairs lobby. Walt, the cigar and candy shop vendor, called to him. "How you doing, Mr. Squick?"

Walt's round face was as smooth as a baby's despite his eighty-two years. He wore a baseball cap over wisps of white hair, and a string tie secured with an elk-horn clip hung from his neck. He liked Squick.

The feeling was mutual as far as Squick was concerned, even if this guy was a Gween. Walt didn't make demands on a person and on top of that he sold the best chocolate in town. His candy was imported from Paris and Rome and Amsterdam. In spite of his appearance, Walt was a connoisseur of fine confections, and people traveled long distances to fulfill their addictions.

"Well, here's one of your chocolate addicts back for a fix," said Squick. "Got any more of those good nut bars I bought yesterday?" He glanced at a newspaper Walt had spread open on the counter.

"Darn shame what's happening to kids in this town," said Walt. "I got fifteen grandkids myself. Glad they all live out in the country." He reached under the counter and handed Squick his chocolate bar. "This one's on me," the old man said. "You look kinda low. Anything wrong?"

Squick muttered an abrupt thanks and turned away. As he crossed the lobby, he stuffed the chocolate bar in his mouth, wadded the wrapper and made a basketball shot toward a nearby trash can. He missed. *Damn Gweens . . . damn . . . damn.*

CHAPTER ELEVEN

The Nebulons are becoming nebulous.
                            —Dark Ch'Var wit,
                              typical of the breed

With all the technology at his disposal, Director Jabu Smith had backups for backups and alternatives for alternatives. So it was with electronic communications, and when the beep went off in Squick's ear, the fieldman thought at first it must be his sleep alarm.

A hazy image formed in Squick's brain: Director Jabu, in a long yellow-and-blue-striped insulcoat, with deep circles beneath his eyes and more wildness than usual to his black beard. Irrationality there, and anger.

Squick thought he was dreaming, but became conscious of his eyes being open and charcoal darkness in the room. He closed his eyes, and the image of the Director grew clearer.

"With so many time zones involved," Jabu began, "some of you are in bed. To those I say this is not a dream, and I assure others this is not a daydream."

He's using Amoeba One, Squick thought.

Amoeba One dispatched long-range transmitting units from Homaal that sought all fieldmen in the world, somewhat in the manner of amoeba-cams. But Amoeba One had unique features, and the characteristic buzzing he heard was lower-pitched, almost gravelly. He saw a bright ruby midair glow to his left.

Squick yawned and sat up, scrunching a pillow between his lower back and the headboard. With his eyes open, he saw Jabu as slightly translucent, and that suited Squick. It seemed like a minor act of defiance, keeping his eyes open to diminish the visual effect of the transmission.

"Stand by," Director Jabu said.

Squick remembered something—the damned fire department inspection was due in two days, and he hadn't recalibrated the sensor in the basement yet. Too many distractions, and Peenchay couldn't be entrusted with the task.

Such inspections, like communications from Jabu, were an irritant to Squick, pesky pressures that forced him along certain courses of action, making him jump through hoops, molding him against his will. He resented anyone with power over him, longed for a situation where he might be in charge. If he were Director he wouldn't have to put up with such annoyances.

He tried to visualize the world from the Director's vantage, and suddenly Squick felt very small and very foolish.

The Director cleared his throat. "Some fieldmen have reported a . . . problem, and I want to hear from all of you now. Radio-op me on Channel 162 or speak into the flying transmitters about anything unusual at all. I can take your calls simultaneously."

Should I tell him about my Nebulons? Squick wondered. *He can't be referring to that!*

So Squick lied, and as he spoke into the flying transmitter he reported nothing out of the ordinary. All the while he wondered if he could still produce Nebulons, and this was something that could only be determined in the presence of a Gweenchild. For

Squick and most Ch'Vars, the viral organisms flowed only if stimulated by an imminent extraction.

The image of Jabu disappeared and the buzzing dissipated, but Squick could not return to sleep. He needed to know about his Nebulons, but something told him he should avoid the troublesome Harvey children. Maybe he needed a normal extraction encounter with children in the field. He'd lay here for a while and then go to work as usual, leaving the Harvey siblings where they were.

"Shittah comforts you in life," Squick thought. *"Shittah comforts you in death."*

He shuddered, tried to discard the mantra from his mind.

Maybe I should have Peenchay kill them.

An uneasiness pervaded Squick now when he thought about the Harvey children. The strange extraction of Thomas Harvey's embidium, and the second attempt, a failure, that left the boy screaming . . . then the failed attempt on the girl . . .

Nebulon production is a delicate holistic balance, he thought.

Each extraction attempt on the Harvey children had results more unusual than, worse than, the attempt before. Perhaps he had been unnerved by the sequence of events. And those strange comments from the girl. Where did she obtain her information? If a bluff it was a good one, with authentic-sounding fragments.

Her words rang like a curse in his brain: *"Your Nebulon count is zero!"* Squick felt faint. *"Zero . . . zero . . . zero . . ."*

As Squick lay awake, he planned his day. He would cruise for strays and call on children with impending birthdays, from the lists—familiar routines that would restore his potency. Then, brimming with Nebulons he would laugh in the faces of the Harvey siblings and spray them with icy, spurting Nebulons. Just before turning them over to Peenchay.

A desperate thought occurred to him, that the Harvey children may have been planted by the Director to develop information. If so, it would be a technique different from any known to Squick, but he didn't rule it out.

Director Jabu was a clever man, unpredictable, and he had that powerful Inventing Corps with its secret workings. Maybe the Harveys weren't human, Gween or Ch'Var; could they be bionic, transmitting data to headquarters, damaging data about Squick?

He had brought these children into his field office. Banned conduct. Against the edicts of Lordmother.

I haven't touched them improperly, he thought. *Not so awful what I've done. Peenchay's actions are infinitely worse. But I've known of his deeds, have looked the other way. I'm an accomplice.*

Peenchay seemed to enjoy killing children for his bizarre diet, and took advantage of every opportunity he could. But Peenchay, despite his gruesome misdeeds, had never directly disobeyed a command from Squick. Not yet.

Squick loathed the code of silence he and the Inferior had developed, for it imprisoned Squick within an ancient stream of criminally insane Ch'Vars. He deserved a different, more exalted lineage.

And Squick suspected he wasn't the only fieldman tormented by questions about his mental health, for it seemed too remote a possibility to consider. Lordmother's Way would keep him on the right track, keep him from becoming another Peenchay. He was proud of himself each time he followed Ch'Var Law to the letter.

He became aware of a faint burr of flying sound, and soon the sound dominated his consciousness and became a buzzing that roared in his ears.

"Fieldman Squick!" It was Director Jabu's voice,

and now the image of the Ch'Var leader appeared in Squick's mind as before. ''Tell me about the Nebulons!''

Squick gave a vague excuse to his superior, asked for a little time, a few minutes. Then without waiting for an answer, Squick stormed down the corridor to the game room in which he'd left Emily.

The magic that Emily had absorbed simmered within her, and she realized that if she reached for it too quickly or too soon, its power might overwhelm her senses. Slowly, ever so slowly, seemed the proper way of approaching the memories that stretched back tens of thousands of years. She entered the place within her brain that stored this gift, and she walked on a plain of ice—a small figure bundled in furs pushing against the bitter cold that swept across a barren landscape. She heard the voices of hunters ahead of her, from somewhere beyond her vision . . .

The hunters chanted an ancient song, a vaguely familiar, strident tune that ricocheted through Emily and frightened her.

The enemy approaches! she thought.

The words of the hunters' song filled her, and she went with the words, unable to oppose them: *''We are Ch'Vars, and for us the lit-tle Gween-child. Come, in the na-ame of Lordmo-ther!''*

''No!'' screamed Emily to the wind that tossed her words back upon her. *''No!''*

And Emily understood the depths of the hunters' transgressions, the sanctioned and unsanctioned acts they committed. Even the sanctioned seemed terrible and outrageous, for what right did this Ch'Var Lordmother have to declare open season on the brains of Gweenchildren? By what right did they plunder?

"The flesh of Gween-child, so sweet but forbidden," the hunters sang.

"It's all forbidden!" Emily shouted. *"From now on, all your acts against my people are forbidden!"*

My people . . . Gweens?

Something seemed awry to Emily, and as her words of protest to the hunters were carried off by an icy wind she realized the futility of resistance.

Ch'Var and Gween, she thought. *I am like both but unlike both. How can this be?*

In a terrible vision of searing, white-hot pain, Emily died under a hunter's jagged knife.

Beads of perspiration covered Emily's face. She tried to understand the vision but feared it, feared uncovering information that lay hidden, information she should not know.

The door to her room grated open, and Squick loomed over her. Emily saw another face behind the handsome, angry one he presented to her. The second face was a dim image, a narrow, mean little child countenance with bristly hair and sharp, poorly spaced teeth. Subhuman, it seemed. Emily concentrated on the image, and it solidified and pushed itself closer to her, held out its arms and hissed obscenities.

Startled, her mind withdrew. This child within Squick was not Squick, and she knew this with certainty.

"I want an explanation now," Squick said. "What's all the drivel you were bellowing about Nebulons, about killing them?"

"Exactly as I said, child thief. I've finished them off, finished you off. I've liquidated you, erased you. You're impotent. Why don't you go off in a corner and die, bastard?"

"Don't mess with me," Squick said in a low, threatening voice. "You're teasing, and I don't like that in a child, especially a female child, especially a Gween female child. I might have to punish you."

"You shouldn't have tried to extract from me. Big mistake, and now you're in big trouble."

"You're crazy!"

"So some say. But the Ch'Var Nebulons are one creature, rooted in the same mother weed. I've poisoned the mother dandelion, crippled its tentacles."

The fieldman's mouth took a dangerous twist, a grimace indicating he was near explosion. Emily was tempted to withdraw, to say nothing further, but the ugly memories would not release her and she was powerless to halt her words. "I speak only truth."

"You've played with the Artful Looper too long," he scoffed. "You're only a kid, no more. Your bag of tricks won't work." He turned toward the door. "I'll be back to deal with you."

With Emily locked in the room again, Squick thought, *Lordmother, what'll I tell Jabu? All the Nebulons gone? From my solitary extraction attempt, she poisoned them all? Impossible!*

A ruby-red flying transmitter awaited him in the corridor.

CHAPTER TWELVE

The flesh of the Gweenchild is sweet and
delicate. How are we to resist it?
—Lament of the Inferiors

Squick paced the corridor nervously in front of his
office, rehearsing what he would say to Jabu when
he arrived. There wasn't much time. He heard the
click-shuffle of his shoes on the linoleum and the
spinning scuff at each end of his route as he pivoted
and retraced his steps.

This time the fieldman had an approximate arrival
time for his superior, which should have improved
the situation, eliminating the nerve-racking element
of surprise brought on by Jabu's unannounced spot
checks. But Squick didn't feel better for the information.

There'd been a brief, awkward radio-op conversation between Squick and Jabu, in which Squick
spewed forth some of the startling things Emily had
said. In mid-sentence the Director cut him short and
ordered him to remain where he was.

"I'm on my way," Jabu said.

The Director's tone had been decidedly harsh and
agitated, so Squick wondered if Ch'Var security
troopers would appear to make an arrest. What the
Director already knew was bad enough—the Nebulon snafu and the Harvey children—but the full account would be worse for Squick, much worse.

During one pass of his office Squick glanced

through the partially open door and did a double-take. He halted in his tracks. Director Jabu stood inside, by the desk! The Director wore a cardinal red insulcoat, open at the front, and carried a sheath of papers under one arm.

Squick nearly tripped getting his feet redirected, and made an inglorious entrance. "My Lord! I didn't see you . . . I didn't know! Have you waited long? I've been right outside."

"You're late, you bumbling banana head. *In* your office, I said, not outside, not down the hall. *In!*"

"My Lord, I'm sor—"

"Shut up and listen. Unlike your time, mine is valuable."

Squick's mind raced as he wondered how the Director had gotten there. Fieldmen weren't taught such things, and this one had never dared to ask.

I've had it, Squick thought. *What does this s.o.b. know? Should I tell all?*

At the thought of revealing everything, the fieldman felt a curious, awakening sense of relief, that finally he might clear the burden of both his transgressions and those of Peenchay. The Director couldn't know all, even with the most sophisticated surveillance.

"Now we begin," the Director said. But long moments passed without explanation. Jabu's gaze held firm, and Squick felt very uncomfortable, very guilty.

He told me to shut up and listen, Squick thought, *but he's pausing and staring at me, as if I should say something.* "Uh, I'm afraid Peenchay will kill me. I need protection, My Lord."

"Why would he want to kill you?"

"Because I . . . because he . . . you don't know?"

"Maybe I do."

He doesn't know! Squick thought. *His eyes . . .*

Uncertainty! "Uh, I haven't been under surveillance?"

Jabu frowned, perhaps because his wondrous technology hadn't provided important intelligence on internal operations, and neither had his renowned ability to sense things, to smell out trouble. Or His Eminence might be faking it, to see if Squick would tell all, to see if . . .

But why fake it? Squick wondered. *If he knows, I'm dead, so he doesn't need . . . is it something more I might know, some minute detail he feels could be useful?*

"Why didn't you volunteer information about your Nebulon problem?" Jabu asked. "You should have notified me immediately."

"My Nebulons are lost!" Squick lamented. Gaze lowered, he shut the door behind him and slipped into the room.

"They aren't merely your Nebulons. Never were. Selfishly you've placed yourself first."

Squick felt the penetrating gaze of his superior without looking at it, and slowly, ever so slowly, he raised his eyes to meet the Director's gaze.

In those eyes above the wild black beard Squick saw the layered disappointment of the entire Ch'Var race, going back to Lordmother herself. The beard faded, and hazy female features seemed to take shape around the eyes. A thin face, frail and sensitive . . .

Jabu's voice intruded, and the beard came back into focus. The Director's lips moved slowly, framing words with utmost care. Ch'Var words, the ancient tongue, rolled smoothly and understandably across the tongue, the lips—pure vowels from the depths of the throat, from the depths of the collective brain.

"I have their medical reports in hand," Jabu said, holding up the sheath of papers.

Squick replied in the ancient tongue. "The Harvey boy's too? I was just about to tell you about him. He's in the basement, second room from the sensor.'' Squick's words seemed too rapid to him, too nervous, and they didn't fill the time adequately. The drop-off at the end of his last sentence left too much time for the plethora of additional information he should reveal. Medical reports? Where did Jabu get those?

Director Jabu shoved the sheath of papers under Squick's nose and said, ''Thought you could play Director, eh? Thought you could perform extractions on unusual cases? And don't think I can't figure out why! Nice little deal you'd have, with an unlimited supply of embidiums from one boy, eh?''

He knows! Or is he guessing? Jabu's expression was cold and intense, with certainty framing the eyes and mouth.

''The minute that boy remained conscious after an extraction you should have contacted me.''

Somewhere, imperceptibly, Jabu's words had shifted to the modern tongue—a smooth, compressed transition.

''W-when did you find out?'' Squick stammered in the new tongue.

''Never mind that! Any thoughts I've ever had about you as my successor are dashed. Directors have common sense. Uncommon common sense. They place the interests of our people before personal ambitions.''

He was considering me. Damn, I've blown it!

''A true Director would have known what to do, shit-for-brains! Immediate medical reports on both children, checking for abnormalities before proceeding.''

''You're right.''

''Read!''

With trembling fingers Squick took the sheath, opened it and scanned the reports. Printed letters jumped around, defied his attempts to tame them. "Nothing unusual here," he said presently. "Two healthy Gweenchildren. All s-seems normal, My Lord."

"Oh, it does, does it? Look at the dates of conception!"

"What? Oh." Squick looked through the pages, compared dates, and before he could say anything Director Jabu swung a big open hand angrily, knocking the papers away. They scattered over the floor.

"The identical date, the identical hour, the identical minute, the identical second!" Jabu roared.

"What's that information doing in a—?"

"Directors need more than the usual, as you might have learned if you'd been patient enough to follow the proper channels toward advancement."

"They can't have the same date of conception. The boy is nearly three years younger. It's a mistake."

"I double-checked. No mistake."

"But that's impossible, My Lord. The gestation variance in Gween mothers doesn't—"

"Delayed egg! Think, man!"

Squick flushed, and searching his memory he couldn't quite recall.

"They're fraternal twins," Jabu snapped. "Girl and boy, girl born first."

"You mean Mother Ch'Var? She and her brother were born like that, she first? Wasn't her brother born three years later?"

"Two years, eleven months, three days, twelve hours, twenty-eight seconds later. Brother Epan."

Squick grimaced. "Same as the Harvey children?"

"To the nanosecond."

"But what . . . how . . . ?"

"Emily Harvey is the alpha-mother of a new race, a new mitochondrial Lordmother opposing our race by definition, competing with us for limited resources. And you, with the intellect of an Inferior, try to extract her embidium! When she blocked your Nebulons, she set loose a chain reaction of slippage throughout our people, and all Nebulons in existence flowed into her body, the body of another race! It was such a delicate balance we were trying to hold! Fool!''

"I didn't realize . . . I'm—"

"So you not only loused up your own Nebulons, but everyone else's. It must have been her racial defense mechanism, and you strolled right into it."

"But, Director, our Nebulons were weak, on the verge of failing anyway."

"Idiot! My Inventing Corps was working feverishly to develop substitute viruses. I ordered research because of diminishing Nebulon counts. I could throttle you!"

Squick took a shaky step backward.

"We've been working on artificial embidiums too," Jabu lamented. "Just a little more time. That's all we needed."

"Pardon me for saying so if my opinion is of no use," Squick ventured, "but I think Emily Harvey should be eliminated. She is a frail girl, and I've been able to keep her locked up easily. We could do it in a . . . humane way."

The Director squinted.

Squick: "I understand that lordmothers are deceptively frail when young, but maybe our opportunity is now, before she gets even stronger." Squick chewed on his lip. "Isn't she really only an alphachild now, before she becomes a woman and selects an inseminator? Isn't that when her strength accelerates?"

A faint smile formed on Jabu's mouth. "So you remember something from your lessons, after all."

"The first challenge of all new races," Squick

blurted. "A perishable seed with hostile forces raging all around."

"Bring the girl to me," Jabu ordered.

Director Jabu waited impatiently while Squick ordered Peenchay to bring Emily Harvey forth, and Jabu noticed the exchange of glances between Squick and Peenchay. Something more than simple nervousness there—something rotten, Jabu sensed. He was irritated with himself that he hadn't noticed before, but he'd been busy, extremely so with all the problems of his race. And his Inventing Corps had directed its attention to the crisis, neglecting other matters, neglecting internal security.

Important details have slipped by, Jabu thought.

A short while later the Inferior returned, shaking his jowly head. "She will not come," he reported.

"I didn't tell you to ask her!" Squick thundered.

Jabu detected terror in Peenchay's features, and the assistant continued shaking his head.

"It's all right," Jabu said, pushing by the others to the doorway. "We'll go to her."

The Director led the way down a corridor, then grew confused in the maze of side exits and doors and twists and turns. He motioned to Squick.

"You lead," Jabu said, and realized he'd just revealed the inadequacy of surveillance, or of his memory. There were only a limited number of designs for these facilities, and at one time Jabu had been very familiar with all of them. That seemed long ago, in the irretrievable past.

I'm not handling this well, he thought.

The weakening of the Nebulons was a crisis no Director in Ch'Var history had faced before. It was a peculiar imbalance of events and forces that seemed to have toppled the racial life-support system into an abyss.

I tried, dammit. I wanted a backup system, safe-

guards, and we only had so many resources to apply. How was I to foresee this, the emergence of a new alpha-mother?

The Harvey girl resembled a deadly virus, he thought, opportunistically attacking the weakened immune system of the Ch'Var race. He agreed the girl should be killed for what she had done, but it must not be done rashly.

Peenchay shambled along behind Jabu while Squick led the way. Jabu didn't like the stench of this assistant. Something foul on his clothing, saturating his pores.

I don't like him behind me! Jabu thought, remembering Squick's fear of the assistant. Information to develop there, when time permitted.

What a curse that intelligent, clear-thinking Ch'Vars have to depend on idiot Inferiors, Jabu thought. *But without them, who would take care of disagreeable tasks?* The Director sighed. *It prevents labor problems, I suppose, the sort Gweens have all the time.*

Squick stopped at a closed door, released its lock and thrust the door open. Motioning Peenchay to one side, he ordered the assistant to remain in the corridor.

Jabu noticed Squick's inquisitive gaze, then nodded approval. The Director stepped first through the door.

A brown-haired girl sat on the floor by one wall beneath a miniature theater, and on her lap she worked to untangle the strings of a puppet. She glanced only briefly at her visitors.

Jabu heard the door close behind him and the click of a lock. Foot-shuffling from that direction, inside the room, affirmed to him that Squick hadn't tried anything funny.

Not that a lock could stop me, Jabu thought. *Not the way I travel.*

"I've been expecting you, Director Jabu," the girl said in a voice that trailed away. She finished untangling the puppet, held the control bar high and made it dance—a kicking step, kicking toward Jabu.

Strength there, Jabu thought. *And weakness, in the voice.* He had the odd sensation that he knew this child, this alternate version of his own alpha-mother, and a conviction came over him that he could no more kill Emily Harvey than he could his own Mother Ch'Var. They were the same in a sense, these race mothers.

And he felt something else, something even more troublesome, a feeling that premonition had forewarned him he would know but once in his lifetime. In his position he had no time to pursue this budding, sensuous woman. He had no right either, for she was not of his own race.

I want you, Emily Harvey, he thought, and with a great, righteous push he fought this untoward, unbidden thought, screamed at it within the mouthless entanglement of his mind.

"Ch'Vars with Ch'Vars; Gweens with Gweens!"

There could be no child from such a union. Then Jabu's train of thought came to a grinding, screeching, skidding halt and nearly derailed. His mind rolled, and presently he was thundering down a different track. Emily Harvey was not a Gween! She was the first mother of a new race! What would happen from such a union?

I am old, but do I dare imagine?

"I want you . . . to accompany me to headquarters," Jabu said. Fear and excitement threatened to overwhelm him.

"No!"

"You're worried about the way I travel, the mysteries of ember travel? You've heard of this?"

The girl did not respond.

"I assure you," Jabu said, "it isn't dangerous for you. I can take passengers."

"I'm not going."

"Shall I get Peenchay?" Squick asked.

Jabu shook his head. "Peenchay is afraid of her, petrified. You didn't notice?"

Squick mumbled something, and peripherally Jabu saw the fieldman's feet shuffle uneasily.

Jabu studied the girl's narrow, delicately featured face. So pretty, so perishable. The eyes were the green of an ocean, mysterious and intriguing, concealing within them the contents of a universe.

"Well, I'm not afraid of her!" Squick said. He lunged for the girl, grabbed her collar and held an open hand by her face, threatening to slap her. "See? There's nothing to be afraid of from this one."

"This is no time for foolish impulses," Jabu snapped. He saw no fear in the girl's face. "Let go of her."

Squick hesitated, and his face took on a strange expression. He stared hard at the Director, then did as he was told and moved away.

Through it all, the Harvey girl hadn't flinched, hadn't shown any defense. An icy stiffness to the face, dominated by sea-green eyes that were slow to move and absorbed everything. No details missed.

The gaze moved to Jabu, and he met it as long as he could before looking away. Had she seen through him, to his heart that pounded so wildly? Jabu took anxious, erratic breaths.

"Bring the robots?" Squick queried.

"I've changed my mind," Jabu said. He sucked in his breath as quietly as he could. "Better to leave her here for the moment. Shouldn't take her against her will, though it might be accomplished. The young mother is not physically strong in all ways, and there are unknown effects of my travel methods upon her. Correct decisions must be thought out, analyzed from every angle. I'll bring assistance, the Inventing Corps.''

''Right, My Lord,'' Squick said, the tone of a sycophant.

''I say to you, Malcolm Squick, and hear me clearly, you are to keep her safe until my return. You are not to harm her or her brother or cause these children to be placed anywhere they will be in danger. Your duty is to protect them. Understood?''

''You're leaving me in charge, even though I—''

''You'd rather I turned this over to Peenchay?''

''No, I didn't mean . . . of course I can do better. Thank you, Director.''

''Don't grovel. Give them toys, games. And provide art materials for the girl. It's one of her special talents.''

Emily's gaze twinkled gratefully in Jabu's direction.

Jabu thought for a moment of the unprecedented challenge he would present to his brilliant Inventing Corps, and wondered what they could accomplish after all that had transpired. He tossed a withering glance at Squick, then set in motion the mechanism to leave.

Jabu saw himself through Squick's eyes: the Director glowing bright ruby red, a glow that penetrated all clothing. Without flame the glowing compressed itself to a brilliant ember that flitted about in final inspection and finally disappeared into the puppet theater.

CHAPTER THIRTEEN

"Gween adults are often more childlike than their offspring."
—Section III, page 11,
"Fieldman's Handbook"

Victoria had spent much of the afternoon doing her hair and makeup, making everything just right, and in the dressing table mirror she admired the effect: Her black hair was arranged in a carefree style, with makeup applied so skillfully one would have supposed her skin contained no pores.

The telephone rang, and she lifted the receiver from the nightstand behind her, flipping on the video relay to project her image to the caller.

"Detective Caplan returning your husband's call, Mrs. Harvey," and he appeared on her pic-tel screen from his shirt collar up. He had a wide face and mouth, with the droop-featured expression of an undertaker.

Victoria blinked her eyes rapidly as she listened to him, and her lacquered nails tapped restlessly on the smooth finish of the dressing table.

"I can only repeat what I told your husband yesterday," Caplan said, "when you first contacted us. We've listed your son and daughter as missing. Reasons unknown at this time. Kids get unhappy. They run away from home. We see a lot of this, too much. Your kids have only been gone for a short while."

Victoria's reply was harsh. "My husband is very

upset with the inaction of your department. And because he's upset, I have to pay the consequences for your ineptitude. You should have found the children by now.''

''We're doing the best we can. The leads are scarce and—''

''Try harder.''

''I need more answers first. I realize you're upset about the children, Mrs. Harvey, but I still have questions. Your housekeeper, for example. Yesterday you said she wasn't up to speaking with me. How about today?''

''Mrs. Belfer doesn't know any more than I do,'' Victoria replied, trying to conceal the agitation in her voice. ''She'd tell you exactly what I've told you. She didn't know the children were missing until we returned home. Mrs. Belfer has not seen them since they left with their grandparents for a little drive the day before we discovered them gone. When she got up the following morning, she assumed they'd stayed overnight at their grandparents' home. Now that she knows the circumstances she's . . . gone into shock . . . very ill in bed.''

''That's not quite the way your husband tells the story. He says she's a drunk and a liar, and there's some confusion about a message on the answering machine.''

''Oh?'' Victoria said, feigning surprise. She wished she hadn't turned on her pic-tel screen, for now the detective could study her expressions, every movement, the tapping of her nails. She stopped tapping, lifted her chin to the screen and adjusted the long silk scarf that hung across her shoulders.

''Now, why would you allow a woman like that to take care of your children?'' Caplan asked. ''I'm puzzled.''

''Mrs. Belfer is a fine woman! And as for the answering machine, I found no confusion over messages.''

"Someone conveniently erased the tape."

"I know nothing about that!"

"Of course not. Look, Mrs. Harvey, I have a tough job to do, and I've got to talk with your Mrs. Belfer. Well, what about it?"

"Impossible." *Bats in Belfer's belfry,* Victoria thought, struggling to think of something funny to keep the edges of her mouth turned upward. Detectives noticed things like that, the little things.

"Then I can't do my job. All right, ma'am, I'll have another chat with your husband. He seems a lot more cooperative."

"I just won't listen to any criticisms of Mrs. Belfer."

"That seems odd to me."

"I don't see why."

"Who does she date? Anyone?"

"I don't know any of her friends," Victoria answered in the loftiest of tones. "She's a servant, and I don't permit her to have visitors here. I don't know what you're getting at, Detective . . . whatever your name is."

"Caplan. Just trying to get the facts straight. Did the children have problems in school or with their friends?"

Victoria furrowed her brow, but just a little so as not to wrinkle it too much. "Well, Emily does see a therapist." She glanced at her nails. "I didn't want to say anything in front of my husband, since Emily is his daughter, not mine. He doesn't like to hear unpleasantries about the girl. But she needs a lot of help. I mean, we all know that most teenagers, um, have difficulties. But in Emily's case it's more than the ordinary sort of thing. She has an overactive imagination, concocts bizarre, unnatural things. Just the other day she was talking about bugs in our walls that only she and Thomas could hear, and she had him believing it. Her therapist says her problem is 'reverse patterning' or some such thing. Anyway, she isn't normal.''

"That's all very interesting.''

He's taking the bait, Victoria thought. *I've got to get him off the Belfer kick. Who knows what that derelict might reveal to him?*

"As I told my husband,'' Victoria said, "I think Emily talked her brother into running away. He's actually a much more cooperative child than she, and when his normal imagination is infected with her ravings . . . well, I think it's dangerous to him. I've said many times that Emily should be committed to an institution where she can be watched, and now this.''

"Yes, ma'am. I see.''

"Thomas would never initiate any action to hurt others. Not that he isn't thoughtless at times, most children are, but he's not vicious. And he's a follower.''

"But why would Emily want to take off like that?''

"Who knows what goes on in a sick brain? I'm no psychiatrist. The girl needs confinement. It's obvious she's dangerous to everyone around her.''

"I'll look into that. Now, back to your house-keeper—''

"Can't that wait until some other day? Next week?''

"If we haven't found the children by tomorrow, Mrs. Harvey, I'll be back to see your housekeeper, no matter how she feels. It's that important.''

Damn! Victoria thought as they ended the conversation and closed the telephone link.

In the mirror she saw her eyes narrow and change from lavender to purple-black. Her expression flattened, and her lips twisted into a hateful grimace. "Emily . . . Emily . . .'' she crooned, "and dear

Mrs. Belfer, my old 'friend,' headaches from both of you . . . headaches that must end.''

Victoria tapped her lacquered nails on the dressing table for a long time.

CHAPTER FOURTEEN

"There will be an awakening and those who
rule will fall."
                    —The only unfulfilled
                    prediction of Emily Harvey

Squick sat at the desk in his second office, deep
within the stealth-encapsulated floors of the Smith
Enterprises branch office, puffing his familiar Ch'Var
hound pipe. His plans and hopes had been scattered,
and were as far removed now from his grasp as intelligence from Peenchay.

The Inferior stood before him, shoulders hunched,
gazing insipidly at Squick. A stream of slobber ran
from Peenchay's thick lips and dripped upon the
floor.

"What should we do about this?" Squick queried.
He inhaled deeply of the pipe, and its smoke comforted him only a little.

"Huh?"

"I put this to you, Peenchay. Save my ass, and
yours. How do we do it?"

"I dunno."

"Director Jabu expects too much of me. I can't
be what he expects. I can't do what I need to do to
become—oh, what do you care?"

"I'm not sure how to answer . . . ."

"You know, Peenchay, Ch'Vars have to face a lot
of the same everyday problems as Gweens. Building
inspectors, taxing authorities, incompetent clerks,

fanatics, airheads and neighbors who play their ste-
reos at all hours. You know, I've never thought of
Gweens and Ch'Vars like this before, and maybe I'm
not much smarter than you.''

Peenchay shifted his weight uneasily.

The Director's orders rang through Squick's
thoughts: *"Your duty is to protect them."* Squick
weighed his options, which seemed limited. He ran
his fingers along the smooth teak surface of his desk,
worked at an indentation on the edge.

This Peenchay looks like a wild animal, Squick
thought, *feral eyes, slobbering mouth, the images of
raw Gweenbrain firing across the subhuman synap-
ses of his brain. But he functions in his niche, better
perhaps than I do in mine.*

''What would you say if I told you this whole mess
is your fault?'' Squick asked. He set the pipe in a
holder on the desktop.

''I dunno.''

Squick gazed at the small puddle of slobber on the
floor and said, ''You're salivating.''

''Whuh?''

''It must be snack time.''

Peenchay's eyes lit up, and like an obedient dog
he awaited permission to go and eat.

Squick waved a hand, and his assistant trudged
away.

Ideas began to percolate within Squick's brain. He
remembered seeing a strange expression on Jabu's
face as the Director spoke with Emily Harvey. So
cautious Jabu had been, almost tiptoeing around her.
And his eyes, the way he looked at her. With awe?
Or fascination? Might it have been desire?

Does Jabu desire this child-woman?

And for a time Squick's thoughts took much the
same course as Jabu's had only a short while before.
There could be no child from such a union, from
Ch'Var and—

But Emily Harvey is not a Gween! What is she, then? Our Director wishes to mate with her? Is that it? I'm sure I saw desire in his eyes . . . Emotion overcoming reason in the leader of all Ch'Vars? But there is logic in it, too, for what options are left to our race with our Nebulons taken from us? Jabu hesitated. He's so cautious, hates taking chances . . . I'll bet he's thinking about it!

Squick, with all he had botched in his career, felt he was certain to receive a career-limiting reprimand from Jabu. Even if he guarded this prize hostage well, and even if Ch'Vars received their precious Nebulons back, Squick was to blame for their loss. And if the Director ever learned of certain indiscretions, and those of Peenchay . . . Squick didn't want to face such a future.

He saw only one path to redemption, and he kicked himself for not seeing it sooner. Lordmother, how could he have overlooked it? Now his thoughts leaped like fire sparks. The girl was an alpha-mother, responsible for a new race. She would need to mate with a male.

Why not me?

"The little one is mine," Squick whispered. "I'll be the first male, the father of a new race!"

The fieldman reminded himself of the quality of his genes, and a new plan clicked into place. It felt right. Everything pointed in one direction.

How much time do I have? Not much, probably. One try may be all I get. But Jabu will return to the game room first. I can gain time by moving her.

He remembered the sensor in the basement that needed adjustment for the fire department inspection in Gween-accessible areas of the building, and a clever ruse shaped in his mind.

With his libido afire he burst from his office.

Keep the girl safe. It wouldn't be safe to leave her in the game room while I tend the sensor. Peenchay might get her. So she goes with me to the basement, to the dark, dark basement.

Squick laughed wildly, a great rolling sound that traveled the length and breadth of the corridor, caroming off walls, floor and ceiling. The laugh surrounded him, and he ran with it.

On the floor in the game room with a doll in her lap, Emily heard Squick coming. She heard him before he made his decision to leave the office, before he laughed. Her heartbeat quickened, and her muscles tensed and twitched with the knowledge that he would appear. She concentrated on the music of her body, and the rhythm of her heart slowed, the spasms in her muscles ceased.

Within moments she heard the door squeak open and saw Squick looming in the semidarkness.

"I'm going to take you with me," he said. "I've got to do some minor repairs to the sensor, our alarm system, and I've been instructed to watch you . . . protect you. The only way I can do that is to keep you in sight."

Emily wasn't comforted by his weak smile, heard irritation in his voice and something else there she couldn't quite define. She tried to direct her attention inward, to pry away and inspect Squick's secret thoughts. She had done so momentarily after his attempted extraction, and gazed into his rotten, demented soul, a soul that reflected the evil of his race. But now it seemed an elusive task, like old memories she couldn't retrieve.

A great mass of racial memories flooded her—Gween and Ch'Var—and individual memories, falling stars against a black sky, points of light that flashed by and disappeared before she could take hold of them. Only one thing stood out clear and bright before her—the Nebulons. She knew they were the path to complete knowledge.

Two kinds of humans on Earth, two ways of being, and she had weakened one of those ways. Beyond that her knowledge was fuzzy. *"Ch'Var! Ch'Var!"* voices shouted within. This Squick was one, and Peenchay another, a mutant subtype, and Jabu stood out above all others. He was the leader, the responsible one.

"I won't go with you," she said to Squick bluntly.

"I can leave you here with Peenchay. Is that what you want?"

"I'm not afraid of him." But her inner voice said, *"Fear both, for both are monsters and they mean you harm."*

"Don't fight me, little one," Squick said, holding a half smile. "I'm probably the only friend you have here, the only person who can look out for your welfare. You may not want to trust me, but what other choice do you have?"

"I have my brother. Where is he?"

Squick reached for her arm and yanked her to her feet, causing the doll to fall from her grasp. Emily struggled against his strength, but found herself dragged forward and through the door, out of the room that was beginning to seem suddenly like a sanctuary, a place where evil couldn't reach her.

"I've got to hold onto you, little one, to keep you safe."

Emily stumbled alongside Squick, and he kept her on her feet when she started to fall in the corridor. The door to the stairwell slid open, activated by Squick's body heat, and he noticed that it went up early, when he was farther away than usual.

He dragged her onto the steps and kept her upright, and they began spiraling downward, reaching landing after landing. They exited on the lowest level, and immediately Squick pulled the girl's slim body against his own, front to front.

It surprised him that she did not try to struggle free, and he held her tightly, felt each contour of her body against his own. Lordmother, she was lovely, but only a child, not a woman. His urges threatened to drown him, to bury him in the abyss that he feared. He stared for a moment into her sea-green eyes. The cold of deepest ocean water, a coldness reminiscent of Peenchay's. Couldn't she be a little kinder? *Lordmother, help me,* he cried silently.

Beyond her he saw the lavender lambency of the sensor coming from behind a partition wall, a dim glow from the weakness of the device, from its needed recalibration. But that could wait. This could not.

Keep the girl safe . . . protect her . . .

Squick's grip tightened further, and he felt his physical power over her. When he saw the soft, sweet cheek that she turned from him, he was tempted to place his lips against her smooth skin. He shoved his face against hers and kissed the child-woman with the North Sea eyes. Still she did not resist, and his free hand explored her body lightly, almost delicately, as a lover might do.

He felt her shudder.

Be careful, he warned himself. *This is not yet a woman. But almost.*

His mind battled with his mind. *You can't do this. You'll be dead. Jabu will kill you.* And the girl? Did he really want to hurt her? Feelings welled up within him that he thought had died long ago. What the hell was happening to him?

Compassion was an emotion he'd bottled up and discarded. It seemed to have existed long ago, before the implantation of the embidium he carried within him. The wild boy with jagged teeth. The carnivore. Who had the boy been? It didn't matter.

Squick laughed at compassion. It had no value in this hard world, none at all. Only the strong survived. The strong wrote history, controlled the planet. Ch'Vars! He was a survivor, spawned by his ancestors, and he would spawn strength, a strength that would be remembered for all time.

"We are the superior race!" he shouted. "And I, Malcolm Squick, preeminent. You're not too good for me!"

She turned her face toward his again, and he saw that her eyes were closed. Perhaps she'd decided to cooperate after all. So he loosened his grip on her, and she slid without utterance to the floor.

Lordmother, what's happened? Squick thought.

The girl appeared to be in a coma. Had he held her too tightly or frightened her? Could she be dead? He didn't see her chest moving, and the cheeks were pale. Her skin felt clammy too, but the eyes—closed. Didn't people die with their eyes open? Always? He didn't know.

Filled with panic, he was afraid to touch her for vital signs. Sweat covered his forehead, and he wiped it on a sleeve. His hands felt funny, numb and cold, as if they belonged to someone else or a corpse.

He called for a robot and had it carry her down the corridor into the storage area of this basement level, nearer the sensor.

Afterward, Squick paced back and forth, trying to gather his wits. In one corner of the basement a pile of static-free tarps in varying sizes had been piled, tarps that were intended to cover various computer, office machinery and robotic parts stored there. That was Peenchay's responsibility: cover the items. But it looked as if the Inferior hadn't worked in this area for months, and parts scattered about the cellar remained unprotected, exposed to dust and deterioration.

Still, Squick felt the Inferior's presence. It smelled of him here. Rotting flesh.

A brief, vagrant thought crept across Squick's

mind, that he ought to bury the girl beneath the tarps, walk away and let the weight of the material suffocate her. If she was alive now. But what would he tell Jabu afterward, that Peenchay did it?

The robot waited nearby, a unit that resembled a squat, rolling dunce cap. A red light on its pinnacle blinked slowly.

Squick had it arrange a few mini-tarps into a temporary bed for Emily, and she was placed upon these. When the robot was gone and a pall of quiet filled the area, Squick moved to the girl. Terror overwhelmed him. He had to do something he was afraid to do. He had to discover if she lived.

"Emily," he whispered, and then louder, "Emily!"

She didn't respond, and he slapped her face, shook her and shouted at her. She neither stirred nor moaned, and he felt not a flicker of life in her skin.

Now he touched the carotid artery on her neck. The faintest throbbing there gave him hope, but only a little and not enough. He had failed again, this time more miserably than ever. The historical record would be unkind to him.

He fled the basement, hit the stairway at full speed and took two or three steps at a time. But the stairs seemed endless, and finally, fatigued, he stopped on a landing to recover his breath. Squick's breath came in deep, slow gasps, his heartbeat slowed, and a vision came to him.

Something pursued him at tremendous speed, a monster as big as a planet, and he could not elude it. He remained mired in one spot, unable to go up the stairs or down. A creature rode the monster, a tall boy with bristly hair and dead eyes that stared at him with furious hatred, mindless hatred.

One avenue of escape emerged, and he took it automatically, a trigger in his mind, a bowing, a submission.

GUTA-FLUT!

The sound was unlike the way it had been described in Ch'Var lore. It was richer, fuller, more resonant, and he savored the serenity it promised.

GUTA-FLUT!

Thus shittah suicide was set in motion from within, the physical response of the Ch'Var to untenable situations, to insurmountable problems. He bowed in his mind, the ritual gesture. The delicate Ch'Var nervous system was breaking down, spinning upon itself, consuming itself.

Squick screamed aloud, though he was sure no one heard him and no one cared enough to help him. He was in the first stage of ritual shittah, consumed by a mind that eats flesh, a mind that eats mind. He heard himself sobbing and wailing, but the sounds came from an immense distance, throbbing more faintly than the pulse of Emily Harvey.

"Oh shittah, shittah, shittah . . ."

His conscious self writhed with futile anger, and he felt his bodily systems winding down, accelerating in a direction they had always had, a direction they had been pointed toward since birth. With dull amazement he realized that he lay supine somewhere, as helpless as the girl, with a giant lavender eye high on the wall above him.

And a dim memory came to him from moments before. He had seen Peenchay grinning at him from one corner of the cellar.

CHAPTER FIFTEEN

"Obey our rules, or an Inferior riding a demon hound will eat the thoughts in your brain."

—From a story told
to Ch'Var children

As soon as Squick disappeared from view, Emily rose quickly to her feet. She'd read about passive resistance in a grown-up psychology book from the library, a book that Victoria had taken away from her before she could finish it. "Playing dead," the author called it, "the defense of the weak against the strong." A trick employed by some animals and insects—one that humans could apply when necessary.

She had briefly considered kicking Squick in the groin, to free herself as she had from the boy on the boat. But she had been close to shore when that happened, a distance she could swim. Here she didn't know the way out, she didn't know where Thomas was, and at least one shark swam these waters: Peenchay.

Ch'Var and Gween memories bumped together uneasily inside her head, unfocused fragments that gave her elusive sensations of power . . . sensations apart from the memories . . . sensations about the future, about Emily's particular path into the future.

It was a triggering of Otherness from seemingly unrelated bits of data, from a collection of disjointed ideas that boiled about in her head and gave her a headache. In her first burst of awareness during Squick's attempted extraction, she had learned that Ch'Var Nebulons had been destroyed, and she had reached for further understanding. But understanding crumbled, and she'd spoken of it to the puppets and the cherubic-faced dolls. Now something more was surfacing, in response to her reaching, stretching consciousness.

She wanted to know the purpose of this terrible inheritance boiling in her mind. Was it all from the Nebulons, or had latent memories been triggered, memories that had always been there? She felt alone, too young to be without guidance. But her chronological age seemed out of sync with the hoary Otherness, with the ghostly cloud that filled her brain and seeped into personal experience, subjugating all that Emily Harvey thought she was.

Thoughts of her grandparents and her father welled up. Would she ever see them again, would she ever return to those paths? Even with the obstacle of Victoria, those paths seemed simpler to Emily, almost idyllic, and they beckoned her.

She realized she hadn't moved from the vicinity of the bed of tarps, and thought, *I've got to get away! Squick will return!*

Hurriedly she slid through the lavender semi-darkness of the basement, stopping to peer from behind tarp piles, machinery pieces, posts and partitions. Odors assailed her, a mixture of dust and grease and something sour-sweet and unpleasant, decaying meat. She thought she heard a muffled noise and crouched beside a chair covered with faded, frayed upholstery. Her arm brushed against it, and she recoiled. Grease on her arm, the dead meat odor. She wiped the arm on a tarp.

Evil lived here, in every particle of air and surface, and that strange, eerie lavender color—stronger in intensity off to her left—coming from beyond a partition wall.

She moved toward the light as if drawn to it, and a terrific surge of music pulsed through her body, a "tom-tom-tom, tom-tom-tom," and she realized it was her own blood beating through her veins, expanding them and sending an urgent message.

Thomas!

From ahead noise drifted toward her: a soft shuffle, something being dragged across the floor. Imagination? She held her breath and listened. The noise repeated itself, and she tried to define it, to give it shape and substance. Something large dragging something heavy.

She took a few cautious steps forward. The basement was quiet, and she waited, watched. Nothing seen, and presently, nothing heard.

Squick had mentioned a sensor down here somewhere. Some kind of alarm system that wasn't working right. Could she use that bit of information? Was it truth?

When she'd first arrived on the roof of this building, her view of surrounding structures had told her the building was many stories high. And later she overheard Squick say there were sublevels, secret levels beneath and between the areas traveled by Gweens, areas unknown to Gweens, the enemy race. When had she heard these things? Had she actually heard them or . . .

The building seemed like a maze, a microcosm of the structures forming in her mind.

I'm somewhere beneath ground level, she thought.

Wondering about the sensor and how well it worked, Emily measured each step she took until she reached two large wooden boxes set side by side. Here she crouched and used the slit between the boxes as a window. She could see around the partition now, and at the top of a wide wall she saw a gigantic Cyclopean eye, or what appeared to be an eye, an electronic oval of lavender and white within folds of dark metal.

Rising from her crouched position, Emily saw with surprise that Squick was lying on the floor, face up. His eyes were open. She sucked in her breath and held it momentarily.

Suddenly Peenchay appeared from one side, and without seeming to notice her he stood over Squick and chuckled, an ominous sound. She wondered at the Inferior's purpose. Had he killed Squick? That thought curdled all hope of escape. If the man could kill his master, why not his master's prisoners? A chill invaded her.

Inferiors . . . mutant Ch'Var subtypes . . . Inferiors—she hadn't known this name previously, hadn't been aware of it. The word swam atop her consciousness.

Peenchay scratched his chin, ran a tongue across his lips, shifted heavily from one foot to the other. His body seemed to heave and swell inside his yellow onesuit like a huge toad, and from one pocket he removed a thin, wicked knife that he brandished over the still form of Squick. In a rambling, singsong voice, Peenchay spoke to Squick's body.

"Think you're smart and I'm stupid. Isn't that right, Meeeeester Squicko! You're fulla shitto, fulla shitto! Who's stretched on the floor? Not me, Squickaree. Rats in the sewer will eat you up. They won't eat me, Squickaree. Into the disposal with you!"

He lifted Squick by the arms.

Emily pushed closer to the two boxes that concealed her and accidentally dislodged something. A small box thunked down, an echo of sound.

Peenchay's face contorted. "Who did that?" he cried. "Is that you, Mr. Director?"

When there was no answer, he called out again.

"Just liftin' Mr. Squick here to get him some help. He doesn't look good. You want me to leave him here for you to look at?"

Again, no answer.

Peenchay lowered Squick to the floor and made a hasty retreat to one side. He disappeared through a doorway.

Good, Emily thought, *this gives me extra time.*

She departed in the opposite direction and found the corridor from which she'd been carried. Some instinct, some dim awareness, told her Thomas was here someplace. How she knew this was a mystery, but her blood continued to pound the message: tom-tom-tom!

Several doors lined one wall, and she opened two. They were small storage rooms without much inside. In the third room she found Thomas.

He lay asleep on the floor, curled fetally with an arm for a pillow, rumbling in the chain of somnolence that she knew so well. Reassuring sounds. A collection of toy cars lay beside him, and he clutched one tightly in his hand. He was in dreamstate, his mind in an alternate gear, but the sounds were shifting subtly, almost imperceptibly, to unpleasantness.

"Thomas," she said, and she shook him by the shoulder. "Wake up."

He responded with a whimper, and Emily jerked him to a seated position. He seemed groggy but unharmed.

"Wow," said her brother. "I dreamed in weird-a-rama. Horrible stuff. I'm sure glad you woke me up. I saw Booger, and he swallowed me, and—"

"Later," she snapped. "We have to hurry. Don't talk, don't argue. Let's go."

With considerable effort she hefted him to his feet, and he stumbled momentarily. They ran down the corridor to the stairway Squick had brought Emily down.

Emily froze in her tracks, hissed: "Listen, someone coming down the stairs!"

The children reversed direction, back along the corridor and out into the room with the lavender eye. Squick still lay on the floor, a loose sack of bones, just as Peenchay had left him.

With a suddenness that palpitated Emily's heart, Peenchay emerged from a doorway she hadn't noticed before. For a moment before the door snapped shut behind him, she saw an array of sparking, colored lights.

Stealth-lock? She thought, remembering Squick's term for the chamber they'd gone through the first day here. *A stealth-lock on this level too?*

A squat, troll-like form, Peenchay walked in a shambling fashion, arms swinging loosely at his sides, hands curled into claws, mouth open, eyes bulging. He moved with deceptive speed, and Emily's panic turned to cold metal in her mouth.

"A way out!" she whispered to her brother. "That doorway, a stealth-lock!"

"The way out is not the same as the way in," Thomas said. "My dream. Panona told me."

The children clasped hands and backed toward the corridor.

"You could do something," Thomas whispered. "We need to go the other way, past him. And someone could be behind us. You can do things with your mind when you want to!"

Emily's breath came in deep gulps. "I don't know what you mean." But she knew exactly what he meant.

Peenchay saw them now, and his movements became more jerky and rapid, and a sucking noise came from his mouth.

Thomas said he heard footsteps and machinery sounds approaching in the corridor behind them, and after a glance in that direction he said two robots were coming, one that walked and one that rolled. Emily heard the sounds, too.

She experienced a core of fear, a dagger of pain that turned to a dull, useless lump in the pit of her stomach. And when she thoroughly understood that this particular fear, this particular path of her mind, was associated with death, the utter futility of their situation angered her. This was unfair, so unfair. She and Thomas didn't deserve to die.

"We're not afraid of you!" Emily shouted.

"Get the Chalk Man," Thomas pleaded.

Deep, buried within Emily, the Chalk Man stirred. She concentrated her attention on him. "We need you," she said. "Protect us!"

And the Chalk Man was born again: a tiny, dim outline against the lavender shadows of the basement, but easily seen by Emily, just centimeters from her face.

"I see it!" Thomas exclaimed.

The Chalk Man moved toward Peenchay and began to grow into a giant, white-etched figure, bolder and with more imposing lines than ever before. He looked back at Emily and smiled, exposing oversized teeth. She urged him on in thought, and with each effort of her mind he expanded as though the breath of her thoughts gave him nourishment, until finally he filled a large section of the basement between Peenchay and the children.

Through the gaps in the Chalk Man, Emily saw Peenchay's toad body halt. He stared with dumb amazement at the apparition before him.

"Leave them alone!" the Chalk Man warned in a blackboard screech of sound.

Peenchay shook his jowels violently, and he rushed forward, beefy arms flailing.

The Chalk Man whirled around behind Peenchay, and before the Inferior could react, the Chalk Man's mouth opened wide and he bent low toward the Inferior. With one gulp he swallowed Peenchay. The victim thrashed futilely inside the void of the Chalk Man's stomach, struggled, scrabbled, scratched. Something bubbled and a great hunk of Peenchay dissolved. One moment he was a writhing toad, the next a lifeless blob. The blob bubbled back up into the Chalk Man's mouth. The Chalk Man chomped noisily for a while, then spat out what was left of Peenchay: a flabby, armless and legless piece of flesh with part of a head.

"You did it, Emily!" Thomas exclaimed, hugging her. "You really did it! I told you you could!"

Emily pulled free of her brother and grabbed him by the hand. "The stealth-lock," she said. "Let's go."

As they ran close to the sensor, it flared to life and became a bright lavender eye, flooding the area in light. It gave off a screeching, whining yelp.

The Chalk Man darted toward the eye on the wall, and the chalky arms and body turned from white to red, forming a line of fire that reached out to embrace the sensor, snuffing its life. The sensor emitted a protesting crackle and a sickly flash of color, then switched off.

The Chalk Man doffed his cap, bowed and walked into the dead eye, where he faded from view.

Safe on the street, Thomas complimented Emily. "Colossal magic, Sis! Can you get us home, too?"

Emily smiled softly. "No, but we can catch a taxi. I've got some money, and if it isn't enough, Mrs. Belfer can pay the difference."

"If she's sober."

They found a taxi-signaling booth, and within moments a robot-operated car came for them.

CHAPTER SIXTEEN

Homaal . . . its existence is my life. Its fire
my heart, its ice my brain.
—Remarks of Jabu

The ember that was Jabu Smith sped through matter
and antimatter, along an infinitely circuitous filament of fire. It sought the icy void within the flaming
ball of creation, a place known in the hearts of all
Ch'Vars—Homaal.

Only Directors and their invited guests actually
traveled to this place, for only Directors learned the
secret of ember travel, a mystical experience in-
duced by certain drugs. None of this was an Inventing Corps gimmick—it preceded all of that—and by
definition the place and the means of getting there
would exist subsequent to invention as well, subsequent to the struggles of men.

It would exist into the infinity of moments.

Although Jabu traveled to and from Homaal and
spent most of his time there, he did not know exactly
where it was. But this did not bother him in the least,
for in the vast scale of cosmology he knew not a
single person, Ch'Var or Gween, who could say for
certain where the Earth itself was.

One thing was like another, just as one thought
resembled the one before it and the one that would
follow. The icy void of Homaal within the flaming
ball—frigid Nebulons flowing within the warmth of
human bodies—these phenomena were along the

knife edge of reality, where the juxtaposition of hot and cold, of life and death, of fear and bravery, of love and hatred, were commonplace.

He felt these opposites each time he journeyed to Homaal, and each time he left. He felt them now.

The great, flaming ball surrounding Homaal must have been the source of the ember that now constituted Jabu, he theorized. It had been a long-standing theory among Ch'Var scholars and philosophers that this ball of fire, if it existed, occupied the center of the Earth, for that seemed to be the closest known place that would qualify. But it might have been instead in the midst of Earth's sun or within any other sun or planet in the universe. Or it might have been in some other place, an unknown place of sight and thought. The drugs did not reveal such things to him.

Jabu felt most comfortable with the center-of-the-Earth hypothesis, and he thought of himself now as a beautifully flaming meteorite or comet, his tiny ember a microcosm of what the larger ball of fire might have been at one time, before it began cooling and formed an outer crust. This was a fear-allaying thought, one that seemed true according to the visceral sensations it imparted.

Actually, he realized the ember might have come from afar, or it might have been in this place, this center of centers, for all time. But if it was within the Earth, it was moving through the universe with the planet and its solar system. A moving center? Shouldn't a center be stationary?

No, it didn't have to be. But he would feel more comfortable if it were. It seemed less safe if it moved.

These concepts were mind-boggling to Jabu, and he considered himself deficient as a scholar or theoretician of such matters. He understood his weaknesses well. The more he considered the possibilities, the more he feared mental and physical breakdown, the stressing of fragile emotions that led inevitably to shittah. Still, the voyages had to be made, and with them went thoughts—rambling, stretching thoughts that one day might attain what they sought.

It would be a perfect joining.

The ember glowed hotter, as it always did when piercing the great fireball from whence it came. Jabu feared these times most, for it seemed to him that fire naturally wanted to merge with fire, that in one instance, the final instance known to this sentient, Jabu, the ember would not be able to extricate itself from a greater force.

He tried to think of other things in such times.

Some Ch'Var scholars said that Ch'Vars originated off Earth, but this was by no means a unanimous opinion. There were many divisions of opinion over many issues. Even when statements from Mother Ch'Var could be located, they were subject to interpretation and spirited argument.

Mythology held that Gweens preceded Ch'Vars on Earth's surface. But this was not conclusive according to some, who believed this followed the design of the collective Ch'Var brain, to test the planet's surface and develop important information before Ch'Vars formed themselves into human shape. It was well known that a thing could best be fully learned by doing it, however, so in this theoretical postulation the Ch'Vars could not sit back and watch too long. At some point they had to commit themselves.

Theories! The Director laughed, a soundless howling within.

He wanted to scream in fear, for it seemed to him that he had been inside the great molten mass too long, that he would never pull free. Then he sensed coolness, and he felt like a fleck of orange sunset dust, turning gray and cold as the sun dropped beneath the horizon. He felt he should be happy at this, for it suggested he might be piercing the icy core of Homaal, entering. But something was different this time, an element out of place. Those Harvey children.

This speck of dust, this Director in an infinite line of Directors, felt not in control as he should have been. Even though he stood at the helm of the Ch'Var race, he was buffeted by it, and in turn the Ch'Vars were buffeted, even controlled, by forces greater than their own. Sometimes even Gweens seemed superior, and in this among all moments of reflection he found himself unable to place any order to the universe. There was an order out there, at least he thought there was, but maybe he felt this because so many people assumed it. Maybe it was all chaos out there in the distance, and in the foreground, and within his own being.

Cold, so cold in his body. A good sign, but still different than before.

"Ch'Vars and Gweens, these are the races of mankind." Where did he learn that? Too much data in his mind from unknown sources so that it could not be questioned, could not be analyzed, could not be turned inside out for its workings, for its fallabilities.

Ch'Vars and Gweens . . . mankind . . . of course, there had long been theories of alien races, of peculiar sentients that were like humans but unlike them. Was anything at all alien in the universe, or was this concept intrinsically parochial, one that betrayed foolishness, ineffectiveness and insignificance in the perspective of the observer?

He felt a maudlin sense of love for all living things in all places, a desire to embrace all knowledge and experience, and he guffawed at himself for this.

I am only a man, he thought, *despite my position. One more human among the countless.*

He was inside Homaal now, a tiny cooling ember

in a great frigid place, a spot of fire fighting for its brief period of existence, its birthright.

His mind was a stream fed by tributaries of experience, and in the final analysis—at least the final one he could imagine—all logic seemed to wash away into brilliant, mindless colors, into fiery, bursting supernovas and nebulas and pyrotechnics . . . and thence to greenswards and infinite, turquoise seas.

Homaal surrounded him, the known place that was an unknown place, and across the turrets of his fortress he saw little orange, purple and yellow succulent plants growing from the vast ice plain, as if the frozen white were a warm desert, as if the diffused orange glow beyond the pale, translucent sky were a nutrient-bearing sun. This was a sky that should not have been. He smelled jasmine borne on a cool breeze.

He shivered, pulled his insulcoat tight across the front.

The Director turned, and inside his fortress, beyond the glass doors of the balcony on which he stood, he saw Margaret Tung, head of the Inventing Corps, awaiting him. A tall, heavyset Oriental, she wore the blue insulcoat of the Corps, with a gold star cluster lapel insignia.

Jabu always left and arrived on this balcony, and though he never varied this he felt he could if he wanted to. He might arrive inside one time, or on the roof, or on a different balcony. But he always did it this way, the known way, for it comforted him most (if only a little) during the perils of travel.

This fortress was a place of strength and serenity to him, as he imagined it must have been for all who preceded him here.

As if in a dream, the doors opened without seeming to be touched, and he was inside, facing Margaret Tung. She was as tall as Jabu, and he tried to focus on her eyes but could not.

It was always like that here upon first arriving—the dreamstate—and for several moments he would feel like a somnambulist. Now as he gazed upon Tung while she awaited his words he felt an uncomfortable tingling in his brain, as if it were a limb with interrupted circulation, coming back from sleep. The olive pupils of Tung's eyes became clear, and she was gazing steadily at him. A pragmatic woman, she had her own theories about Homaal, and in each of them she tried to rely upon pure science, upon the known. But ultimately, even the most scientific-wrapped theory she came up with was only that, a theory—flawed and unprovable. Mysticism prevailed.

We are magicians, Jabu thought.

Jabu told her now of the Harvey children, of Thomas Harvey's embidium that Jabu carried in his pocket, and of Emily Harvey's wild assertions. He explained why she had not accompanied him, and said, "We must go to her." But he heard a degree of hesitancy in his voice, and he realized he had acted impulsively, assuming that Tung would see the logic of his wishes. She was disturbingly independent, a woman who used her unique, essential talents as an inventor extraordinaire to get her way with the Director.

"Long have we known the importance of the Nebulons," Tung said with an irritating regality, "and as they diminish, my Corps works feverishly to develop substitute organisms. My time is better spent here, continuing the effort. We are very close and should not break stride."

"I understand your concern about the creative process, the way you don't like to be disturbed in the midst . . . and I wouldn't be making this request of you if it wasn't important."

"I must return to my projects," she replied, a hard tone. "There is no point in me seeing the girl, for I can do nothing with her. If she did something to the Nebulons, the viruses, that is beyond my realm. I am laboring for a substitute, and the answer is linked to artificial embidiums. I have nothing to do with real Nebulons, with the Nebulons you say this witch has stolen."

"But you must see her! You must try!"

"What is done is done, My Lord Director."

Jabu wished he had the strength to force his will upon her, but in the battle of wills he had long ago given up any such attempt. Permitting Tung free rein had resulted in a number of astounding inventions that complemented the natural powers of the Directorship. He was grateful she had at least consented to the artificial Nebulon and embidium projects, but she should go an essential step further, acceding to his request.

Request! I should not be making requests of her!

He met her gaze, saw no defiance there, hardly any emotion whatsoever, only the intransigent look of an equal who had made up her mind and would not be deterred.

Her appearance before him whenever he called for her indicated that he might have a slight edge, but it was ever so slight, nearly imperceptible. Still he sensed this advantage and wondered how he might enlarge upon it, and as he stared at her he saw a shift in her eyes, a weakening.

Her eyes hardened again, and she said: "I must return to my work, mustn't let inspiration slip. We're close on both projects, maybe a little closer on the Nebulon project than on the embidiums. The Nebulons must be solved first, I believe, and from that the link to the other."

Jabu nodded, though he began to envision an argument that might sway her, that Emily Harvey might hold a key essential to the invention process. But his words wouldn't cooperate, wouldn't form themselves into a logical order that he could convey.

He detected relief in Tung's expression.

She turned and hurried away.

The frigid interior world known as Homaal was an ice plain that stretched as far as the eye could absorb in all directions around the ancient rock fortress Lordmother had built, which according to legend stood at the plain's precise center. Jabu did his best thinking away from the fortress, far out on the ice plain, where the crispness of the air cleared his thoughts, aligning problems in neat orderings that allowed him to prioritize, dealing with the most essential first.

With his insulcoat secured tightly around him and the hood snug, he leaned forward on the ice-cycle, peering through the windshield. This vehicle speeding across the white plain resembled a motorcycle, but instead of tires it had two narrow parallel skids, with friction belts on the bottom of each that made purchase on slick surfaces.

He glanced back, and the gray stone turrets of the fortress were just above the horizon, with the main portions of the walls out of sight. Jabu looked forward again and spun a tiny finger gear on the handlebar, increasing the vehicle's speed and causing wind to whip hard around the windshield, slapping cold air against his face.

How to deal with Margaret Tung . . . Such a stubborn woman, and though she would never admit it she had limitations, important limitations. She didn't have all the answers, and sometimes Jabu pushed her to admit her ignorance. She didn't know, for example, where the oxygen in this tiny, enclosed world came from. Always the admissions came slowly and reluctantly from her.

Jabu made another finger-gear setting and then another, until the maximum speed had been reached and the cold wind was fierce against his face. Soon the fortress could no longer be seen behind him. He brought the vehicle to a stop and swung a leg over to disembark.

From a carrier on the rear of the ice-cycle he removed a thick, soft tahnchair pad, which he placed on the ice and sat upon.

He gazed away, past a foreground of succulent orange and purple plants, into a nearly featureless distance. He had never gone farther than this, just beyond the horizon of the fortress, and neither had anyone he had ever heard of. Curiously, though it seemed illogical, he harbored no interest in what lay beyond, and he wondered why he felt this way.

Fear? He felt a little now, he thought, but not much, more a selective disinterest about this particular unknown. He could not remain focused on the subject, and soon it slipped away entirely.

Lordmother walked here, according to the teachings, and Jabu felt her sacred energy flowing through him, sorting priorities. The continuance of the Ch'Var race emerged above all, the essential of essentials, but in its path he saw a mammoth, ghostlike image of Emily Harvey, preventing a long, thin line of Ch'Vars from advancing into the future.

He struggled, a mental tug-of-war, and with the force of concentration he partially scattered the image of the Harvey girl. Through the fragments of her countenance he envisioned all Ch'Vars happy, with manufactured or cloned embidiums in every brain and an unlimited supply of artificial Nebulons. His people had no worries of any kind.

Perhaps Margaret Tung was right in her own way, within her limitations.

Now the image of Emily Harvey returned with ferocity, scattering his halcyon vision to dust. And this time no amount of effort could clear his mind of her.

Emily Harvey's mouth formed a lover's smile just for him, and this so frightened and unnerved Jabu that he leaped on his ice-cycle and fled across the plain, toward the security of his fortress.

CHAPTER SEVENTEEN

Motives: In all acts, in all times, in all people. Beware!

—Romuri, the first Director
chosen by Mother Ch'Var

Emily and Thomas managed to scrape up enough money for their cab fare home. When they arrived, Emily counted out the money carefully and paid the robot driver, a friendly machine that made no comment about their disheveled appearance or the fact that it had picked them up in a rough part of the city. Nor did it object when they gave it an enthusiastic thank-you in place of the tip usually earmarked for the Robo-Cabbies Educational Fund.

As Emily and Thomas walked up the long stone pathway that led to their front door, apprehension seized her. The house lay in sunset shadows and seemed less like home than ever before, and she realized she no longer wanted to live there. No longer could she tolerate Victoria or even Mrs. Belfer, and in an alarming twist of emotion she felt herself building a wall between herself and her father. Emily felt like giving him an ultimatum, forcing him to choose between wife and daughter.

I'd lose that confrontation, she thought.

And she described her feelings to Thomas.

"The old house looks the same to me," Thomas responded from the top of the stairs. "I think things will be fine, even with Victoria. It will smooth out if you give it a chance. You're just tired."

Emily thought her brother might be correct. They had been through a terrible experience that would take time to recover from, to set it in perspective. She wouldn't get all of her rest in one night. She tried to set negative thoughts aside, but when she crossed the porch she thought of Gweens and Ch'Vars, of the mystery she had been exposed to through Nebulons or drugs or both. She had seen no mention of these racial divisions in books, magazines, newspapers, on television or on the radio. None of the adults or children in her life had ever mentioned such people. But she had information on them in her mind, flickering bits of data that pulsed and receded, just out of her reach for the moment but approaching, inexorably approaching.

"I feel so peculiar about what happened," she said, "like . . . like something's hatching within me."

Thomas giggled as he turned the door handle. "What are you going to do, break through your outer shell, peck your way out and turn into a weird alien? I'd like to see that. My sister the lizard-woman."

She nudged him playfully, but didn't feel that way inside. Nothing bothered Thomas for long, if at all. He'd floated through the experience like a charmed person, unaware most of the time that evil forces were raging around him.

Lucky Boy, she thought, remembering her nickname for him.

Her brother soared with ideas and dreams, it seemed, even in the instants of emergency when he'd helped her produce the Chalk Man that rescued them. Emily seemed cursed with the burdensome task of seeking explanations for puzzles that didn't want to be solved. Ch'Var and Gween memories stirred again within her: dim, ineffable thought forms.

Mrs. Belfer greeted them at the front door, red

wig askew, eyes bleary from alcohol. Her cheeks puffed from the sides of her face like miniature pillows daubed with pink paint.

"Whazzis?" she said, and wrapped her fat arms around the children. "My babies are back," she sobbed, and tears ran down her face.

Emily was touched by the housekeeper's greeting, and some of the negative feelings she'd experienced while approaching the house retreated. But not for long.

"Look who's here!" Mrs. Belfer shouted when they were in the living room. "Oh, Victoria! Come out, come out, wherever you are!" She laughed at her own silliness and glanced at Emily. "Your stepmom's been really, really worried about you. Could barely make it to the boutique yesterday."

Mrs. Belfer laughed again and coughed on her own saliva. She grabbed a brandy bottle by the neck and stumbled from the room, muttering as she went, "But your poor dad's really broken up about you, yes indeed."

I need to get out of this zoo, Emily thought.

Victoria's familiar voice filled the room with unwelcome sound. "Mon Dieu, look at the filthy urchins! Where have you been for two days? We've been worried sick, and the police are out searching every place. Do you realize how many people you've inconvenienced?" She threw herself on the couch, curled into a feline pose.

"We got kidnapped," Thomas said. "By that guy who was going to give me the free party. He wasn't so bad at first. He took us to this place that had all kinds of neat things—gold toys and stuff, this neat-o train. But then things got weird and I saw Booger . . . in a dream, I think. And there was this monster named Peenchay, but Emily's Chalk Man chewed him up and we got away."

Victoria stared at the children, her eyes filled with cold disbelief. "What an outlandish story."

"He's telling the truth," Emily said. "We were in a scary building on the other side of town, way underground." Emily paused, realizing that in her rush to escape she hadn't taken time to notice the address of the building, street names or landmarks. It could be hard to find.

Victoria snorted, and her eyes were narrow lavender slits. "Likely story. Do you know what I think, Little Miss Crazy Brat? I think you talked your brother into running off just to cause trouble between your father and me. Your strange ideas are infecting your brother, and you've put him up to the most outrageous story I've ever heard. A kidnapping! Come now! Where did you sleep, in the city dump? And how did you get home?"

"Taxi," Thomas said. "The building we were kept prisoner in had stealth-locks, mole-tubes and a bizarre electronic eye."

Victoria shook her head in dismay, and her long locks bounced gently with the motion, returning to perfect position. "While I've worried my head off, here you two are gallivanting around town, making up wild stories."

She lifted the phone and tapped one of the blue programmed buttons. "I'd like to speak to my husband, Dr. Patrick Harvey." A pause. "I don't give a damn if he's going into surgery or not! This is urgent!"

There was another pause, and then Victoria's voice grew softer, sensual. "Patrick? The children are all right, they're home. I'm sorry I interrupted you, but thought you should know. They aren't hurt, but they're telling incredible stories, lies. They ran away, Patrick, I'm sure of it. I see it all over Emily's face. I've warned you over and over, and now the girl is ruining the boy. It's time to have her institutionalized."

A burst of angry noise shot from the phone, and Victoria's face filled with color.

"Don't you dare speak to me that way!" Victoria screamed. She slammed down the receiver and turned in Emily's direction, chin out. "See what you've done? We got along fine when you weren't here. I'm not going to let you ruin my life, you freaky child. You're not going to spoil this marriage with your little schemes and cabals. Thomas, upstairs and take a bath!"

Thomas ran from the room, and Victoria glowered at Emily. "It's time for a little chat," Victoria said.

"I've nothing to say to you."

"Then listen. You're a lying, sick-minded little *merde,* and I'm going to make certain you never cross me again. Understand, little bitch?"

"I do, but you don't," Emily answered in a tight voice. Anger threatened to overwhelm her, and she fought off an image of her Chalk Man chewing Victoria into little pieces and spitting them out like watermelon seeds.

"You're going with me to see the Harvey children," Jabu said to Margaret Tung. He patted one pocket of his insulcoat. "The boy's embidium is here, and I'll bring it. Select a small travel crew to accompany us, and pack whatever equipment you need. Be ready in an hour."

"But, Director," she protested, "our work is here. We can't just—" She paused, looked at him quizzically.

Tung stood before a gray and white computer bank that fed into a row of test tubes, giant and miniscule, arranged in order of size like the pipes of an organ. Workers in blue insulcoats hurried about from the tubes to computer terminals, making adjustments, removing fleshy items from the tubes, placing items in the tubes, conversing with one another in hushed, serious tones. This was one of the fortress chambers used by the Inventing Corps, a gray rock room without windows that had only one door in and out.

Jabu grabbed her arm and shook her, and her features became startled.

"No discussion," he said in a level, hostile tone. "I'll return in an hour. Be ready. You and no more than four others. We'll start with the Harvey girl. I want an on-the-spot report from your team."

"We aren't psychoanalysts or physicians," Tung said. She pulled free, but Jabu detected fear in her eyes. The mouth was a narrow, quivering line.

"Bring the correct equipment, select the correct people. You've got the resources here. I know you do, so don't try to snow me. I'm not entirely ignorant of your operations, and know the medical backgrounds, the deep research your people have done."

Tung stared at the floor.

"Are you there, woman?" he demanded. "Do you understand what I'm saying to you?"

"Director, if we leave the Nebulon and embidium synthesis projects, we may not be able to resume them. The creative process is fragile—it isn't all in the computers and retrievable. We're in the midst of something now."

"I don't care. Do as I say!"

"Yes, My Lord Director."

In a single trip Jabu transported himself and the Inventing Corps contingent along the filament of fire between Homaal and the surface of Earth. They were six embers speeding along a circuitous void, and when finally they emerged it was before the supine form of Malcolm Squick.

The fieldman's eyes were open and lifeless, staring into the dead eye of the sensor, death absorbing death.

Margaret Tung touched Squick's neck and rubbed one of his temples with a forefinger in the ancient way of her people. "He's barely alive," she said. "Shittah, stage five."

"Praise be to Lordmother," the workers said reverently.

Squick's eyelids fluttered.

"He's fighting to the surface of consciousness," Tung said. "The last surge before death."

"Body over here!" one of the Corpsman yelled from Jabu's left. "It's the Inferior, Peenchay. He's gone, and it wasn't self-inflicted."

Jabu didn't look in that direction. Impulsively he brought forth the vial containing Thomas Harvey's embidium and swallowed the whole thing, vial and embidium, staring all the while into Squick's eyes.

In the Director's stomach, the gel-glass of the vial dissolved immediately, and he knelt over, laying his hands on the dying man's face.

Jabu became entirely still, and he heard not a sound or a whisper from any quarter. Beneath the surface of Squick's skin, far beneath, he felt a movement approaching, ever approaching, like a seismic tremor dispatched from the core of a planet.

Jabu absorbed the motion in a tremendous, trembling seizure, and it consumed him. The surging life spasm commandeered Jabu's life energies, plunging him back into the depths of existence, to the last breath, the last heartbeat. Plunging, ever plunging went this soul known as Jabu Karuthers-Smith into the soul of another and beyond, far beyond, toward eternal stillness.

In the last nanosecond of existence, at the death point of all life, Jabu surged and emerged, and with him came Squick and another, a Gweenchild bearing both of them. A faceless, soulless, memory-less

Gween embryo brought them back and then broke away from Jabu, merging with Squick. And from far behind, screaming in the darkness, came another child on a weasel-hound, a boy with bristly hair, jagged carrion teeth, and mean, twisted features. The image shriveled and blackened.

Jabu felt something warm on his neck, a hand, and the image of Margaret Tung formed in his mind, an image that shapeshifted in a haze of swirling water into Emily Harvey, a sea-witch.

The Emily Harvey image spoke in the voice of Tung: "Director, are you all right?"

The image exploded, a sunburst that hurled fiery fragments through every pore of Jabu's body.

The hand on his neck felt cool now, and his body was every burning life ember of every Ch'Var, and another voice slipped through.

"Squick is alive," the voice said. "Shittah reversed! How can it be?"

Jabu's hands became icy, and the force of cold went through his body, repelling heat. Equal forces. And the Director's body became the water-bearing form of a Ch'Var, barely warm—a fragile organism severed from the Lordmother and left floundering, gasping for life.

The dead eye of the sensor filled Jabu's soul, and the sensor eye flickered on above him in a lavender, sickly glow.

Faces appeared between Jabu and the sensor, and moist, warm hands were on his face—Squick's hands. And Squick's face beyond, closest to his. Where Jabu had been, Squick was, and where Squick had been, Jabu was, and Squick was the more energetic of the two.

But no one spoke of this, as if it hadn't happened.

Jabu pushed Squick away and rolled into a fetal position. Presently Jabu fought his way up to his knees, breathing hard.

"Are you all right, Director?" Squick queried.

"I'm fine, fine."

"You shouldn't have done that," Tung said, staring at Jabu with concern. "You implanted the Harvey boy's embidium in Squick, didn't you?"

"How did I get on my back on the floor?"

"We couldn't see. There was a blinding light around you and Squick, white-hot, and when it dimmed you had exchanged positions with him."

"I've never been through an implant like that," Jabu said. "Never attempted during shittah five, so close to death, and never with such an embidium."

"What do you mean?" Tung asked. "Such an embidium?"

Jabu didn't answer but tried to regain his breath.

"Something wrong with the embidium?" Tung asked.

"Maybe there is, I'm not sure. I thought I was lost in Squick's death dance, and then I came back . . . we all came back . . ."

"Whatever that embidium is, it's in Squick now," Tung said. "He looks pretty good now."

"You gave me the Harvey boy's embidium?" Squick asked, his face radiating fear. He too was on his knees and staring.

"You would have died," Jabu said. He felt better, and his breathing became more regular. "I sensed that I had to save your miserable life, and then . . . there was something else, a terrible creature that died as I watched. Old memories, I believe, from your first transplant. These new ones are strong, overpowering."

"Yes?" Squick said.

"I didn't have a will of my own, I had to do what I did for you, like—like the embidium had a mind of its own that directed my motions."

One of the Corpsmen snickered.

Jabu smiled. "A mind of its own. Of course it has

a mind of its own, but it wasn't implanted in my head and wasn't supposed to . . . I mean . . ."

He glanced at Tung, then back at Fieldman Squick. "Time's wasting," Jabu said. "Where's the Harvey girl?"

"First room," came the response from Squick. As he pointed, he seemed to see for the first time the mangled, lifeless body of Peenchay, identifiable by the ripped yellow remains of his onesuit. "What the hell?" Squick said.

"You don't know anything about that?" Jabu asked.

"N-nothing. The boy's in the second room."

CHAPTER EIGHTEEN

> Freedom is a wild, uncivilized state. Like
> children, my people need discipline, an iron
> hand. Thus do they know they are loved.
> —From the *Sayings of*
> *Lordmother Emily,* cloth edition

Squick's hands tingled, and he had an imprecise image of laying them upon someone's face—upon Jabu's? Fieldman and Director knelt, staring at each other, recovering their breath.

No, Squick thought, these hands had been upon his own face as he lay where Jabu knelt now, and they had not been Squick's own hands at the time. But how could that be, these appendages that were not always his own?

A blinding light around us—white-hot. What happened?

And a fresh Gweenchild embidium touched his thoughts, with new childhood memories that were meshed with his own. He felt the excitement of newness, of freshness, and all his senses seemed heightened, perfected.

Something had been failing with the first implant, the wild boy, for Squick had not been happy. He recalled seeing the image of the wild boy shrivel and blacken, but could vestiges of the implant remain?

He tried to separate new from old and personal from implanted, but could not. A piece of information he should not have known surfaced, a name.

Thomas Harvey! Another followed, Emily Harvey, fainter than the first. Such details were supposed to be gone, Squick reminded himself, washed away to prevent conflicts with other recollections, other experiences.

I have the embidium of Thomas Harvey. Tom-Tom!

Squick pressed for other details but detected no names or dates or addresses. Just faces, ghostlike faces and smiles, and a vague sensation of happiness, of contentment. No need to explore that realm, to pick at it. The sensations were perfect as they were and should be left alone.

He felt a new contentment, an awakening serenity, and sighed. He gazed around upon the others present, and his thoughts fled. When he looked upon the faces that went with the voices, the voices became visual—blinding, throbbing spotlights.

He stared into the lights that should have been faces, and each light became a frosty white fingertip, with a million eyes upon each fingertip, like subatomics on the head of a pin. Each finger saw all . . . the eyes of each were the eyes of all, and from them flowed the icy Nebulons of a collective organism.

Squick's hands tingled again, and an infinite queue of Gweenchildren marched before him, with their skulls peeled away, brains exposed. He wanted to reach out to them, to all of them, begging them for forgiveness. But they marched on as if he didn't exist, as if he had never existed, and he knew his efforts would be futile. No matter what he did, it would be utter futility.

Despite all, despite his immense and eternal sadness, Squick felt instilled with a fresh and vibrant sense of urgency, fused with optimism. There could be different ways from past ways, but what might they be? Who might suggest, and who might lead?

His head felt heavier but better, with more desirable elements on the surface for his use, and the darker, past ways inundated, buried beneath a hot lava flow of New, of Different.

Hello, Emily Harvey, he thought. *I am your brother now.*

"They aren't here," a voice said. "The children are gone!"

Squick saw the speaker, a stocky man in a blue Inventing Corps uniform, a short distance down the corridor from the sensor. The second door was open, and the man looked very agitated. A nearer door was open, too, the first from the sensor.

"Gone?" Squick felt the word vibrate across his lips. He cleared his throat. "But they . . . the girl . . ."

Squick recalled that she had gone limp as he tried to attack her, and he remembered his subsequent flight from the room in terror. He'd left the door open, then gone into the seizure and the shittah death dance beneath the sensor. For a long time he had stared into the sensor eye.

"Search the building," Squick said. "They can't be far away."

The image of the dead sensor flashed in his mind just as one of the Corpsmen said, "The stealth-lock down here is out of whack."

Tied in with the sensor! Squick thought. *They've escaped!*

"The s-sensor n-needed adjustment," Squick stammered, "and with the press of events I delayed it. I didn't think—I mean, security was functioning, except for the fire and burglar alarms in the Gween areas, the property management offices. What have they done to Peenchay? How could they—mere children—do this?"

Squick recalled the terrible transgressions of Peenchay, and of his own, and he was deeply ashamed.

Director Jabu ordered a search of the building,

and Tung issued specific assignments to the Corpsmen. All of the Corpsmen left, including Tung.

"This wasn't entirely your fault," Jabu said in a tone so kindly and without intensity that it surprised Squick. Flat words, soft words. "There are other forces at work here. Forces we may never understand."

"I was beginning to realize that," Squick said. "It was overwhelming me. I couldn't cope. No one could."

He caught the Director's disapproving gaze, and Squick added quickly, "Other than yourself, of course, My Lord."

"Don't patronize me, Malcolm."

"Sorry." Squick lowered his gaze. *Malcolm? He's never used my first name before.*

"And don't grovel. I've always thought you were special, Malcolm, beyond your extraordinary Nebulon counts and excellent record of filling orders. Your rebellious strain—"

"I'm sorry, uh, I thought I was—"

"Quiet, man! Your rebelliousness is an asset, a requisite for leadership. Without it you're no more than a follower, but it must be structured, controlled. Curiously, it takes a rebellious nature, almost iconoclastic at times, to fit into the top of our establishment. It has always been this way, a paradox it seems sometimes, but this is one of the facets all Directors have looked for in choosing successors."

"And that is why you saved me?"

"It's not in the bag, man!" Jabu smiled, just a little.

The two men rose to their feet simultaneously, holding gazes with each other. To Squick, the Director seemed less massive than before, more approachable, more human.

Squick wet his lips, resisting the urge to ask questions. Could it be? From the edge of death to this? He heard voices on upper levels, with doors opening and closing.

"There are several candidates I am considering," Jabu said, "and among them, you. In many ways I like you best. You were ill . . . those near infractions with children, I am aware of them. Even worse, you looked the other way while Peenchay ripped donor children apart. I saw your soul in the midst of the blinding white light no one could look upon. I wanted to disbelieve what I saw, and I experienced your worries, your attempts to be good, to follow Lordmother's Way properly . . . Oh, Malcolm, how my heart goes out to you! That implant, that insane wild boy. I'm so sorry that something went wrong. I blame myself for the choice of that implant, though I don't know what I could have done differently. Systems are not infallible, and neither are people."

"That's okay. I don't hold you responsible."

"Part of it has to do with the ancient weakness of our people, the weakness Inferiors are least able to control." His voice dropped to a whisper. "Gween-meat. You know what I mean only too well, and the tendency touches us all. It contributed to your problem, and the defective embidium only made matters worse. You were unlucky. But rest assured, I believe you are cured."

"Entirely?"

"I sense that you are. As a result of the newest implant, of the journey we took in the blinding light of death and life. But only you can answer that question with certainty. In time the answer will be known."

"If I am cured, what a joy! I had so hoped, oh, how I had hoped! But My Lord, what might I become Director of? The Nebulons are gone, and all is . . . I don't mean to be pessimistic. I'm just trying to be realistic. Won't our race die now, since we can no longer make the embidium extractions needed for Ch'Var mental health? What is left, My Lord?''

"There is always something left." Jabu's gaze became penetrating, and he added, "Are you afraid you might be the last Director?"

"No, it isn't that."

Jabu told Squick of the researches of the Inventing Corps into artificial Nebulons and embidiums, of having to force Tung away from that process, and of her comments that her creative focus might be irretrievable.

Tung returned with her men while Jabu was talking about her, and after a moment's pause she reported that the children were nowhere on the premises.

Jabu led the group through the disabled stealth-lock, and they became seven flying embers.

CHAPTER NINETEEN

> A death clock ticks in the human body and
> in every race of man. One day our race will
> end, and a new one shall rise.
> —Words of Mother Ch'Var

As soon as Emily had gone to her room, Victoria
walked swiftly toward Mrs. Belfer's back porch
room. Angrily, Victoria slammed the door open
against an inside wall, and flecks of plaster scattered
on the carpet.

The room was messier than usual, with newspapers, food wrappers, magazines and romance novels
strewn about. The odors of alcohol and cheap perfume mixed in the air. Victoria wrinkled her nose.

Mrs. Belfer sat up on her bed of lace pillows and
demanded in a drunken slur, "What you doin'? How
about knockin', the finishin' school way?" She
raised one pudgy fist, and with a slightly bent wrist
made three delicate little taps against the air before
slumping back on one elbow. She stared insolently
at her visitor.

Victoria glanced around, saw a pile of empty wine
and brandy bottles in the sink, with dirty dishes piled
around. "I don't have to knock in my own house. I
do as I damn well please here. Get out of that bed."

"Make me."

With hardly a missed beat, Victoria clenched her
teeth and dove into combat, pulling away Mrs. Belfer's red wig. Victoria's other hand seized a handful

of the thin, dark hair that sprouted in uneven patches from the housekeeper's pink scalp. She pulled Mrs. Belfer to a standing position, in terrified attention.

"Aw right, aw right," Mrs. Belfer slurred. "You don't hafta get nasty."

"Everything's falling apart and it's your fault!" Victoria roared. "If you'd watched the children as you were supposed to, none of this would have happened. They wouldn't have run away and caused me all this." She shook Mrs. Belfer and then released her.

"We've been through this," the slovenly woman answered in a sullen tone. She stepped backward, retrieved a bottle of white wine from the floor by her bed and edged toward the open door.

But Victoria grabbed her arm and shrilled: "Don't leave until I'm finished with you! Patrick says I'm never to say anything against his brat Emily ever again."

"That doesn't sound like the doc, callin' his kid a brat."

"You stupid old woman, of course he didn't call her that. Don't play with me! Mon Dieu, when I think of all the oddball statements that girl's made, and he keeps on defending her."

Mrs. Belfer tipped up the wine bottle and took a generous swig. "Well, I don't see any reason to get so upset. Man's got a right to say what he wants where his own kids are concerned."

"Who cares what you think? You're nothing, a broken-down loser. Patrick says he's going to divorce me if I don't straighten out. That sonofabitch is threatening to divorce me because of you!"

Mrs. Belfer took another drink of wine.

"Did you hear what I said, the way he talked to me? What are you going to do to fix the mess you've caused? Talk to Emily for me, get her to admit her lies." Victoria felt her lips compress into a tight, smug smile. "Yes, that would solve it. The girl listens to you. I'll even slip some extra cash into the deal for you and the girl."

Mrs. Belfer shook her head. "Oh, I could never do that. She's a good girl, won't turn out like you."

"Aren't you forgetting your place in this little arrangement, that your position depends upon me?"

Another swig of wine. "I don't care 'bout none o' that."

"You'll be unemployed, out on the street."

"So what?"

Victoria pushed her face close to Mrs. Belfer's, despite the odor. "We'll work something out," Victoria purred, "so you can continue to buy your bottles of booze. Quid pro quo: you help me, I help you."

"You think I'm just a lush you can push around, don't you? Well, maybe I got a surprise for you." Mrs. Belfer licked her lips.

Victoria wrinkled her nose and thrust the housekeeper away from her. "You smell like a skid row bum."

Mrs. Belfer lifted her wig from the floor and set it backward upon her head. The wig slid askew and gave her a clownish appearance, but she pulled herself erect and glared at Victoria.

"I like those kids," Mrs. Belfer said, "and I like the doc. You're no good for them, and I'll tell about the girl you let drown at your college party. I'll show the videotape I have, and I got lotsa copies made of it, spread 'round town in safe places. Society page headlines, I can see 'em real clear."

Victoria felt her face flush. With shaking hands she removed her long scarf and stretched it tautly between her hands.

Mrs. Belfer's eyelids narrowed, and she hefted the bottle to one side, like a weapon.

A black rage consumed Victoria, and she moved

toward the housekeeper, rolling the scarf into a tight rope as she approached.

In her bedroom upstairs, Emily slipped into a clean sweater and skirt and combed her damp hair. In the mirror of her dressing table, she saw herself, slight-figured with straight brown hair . . . and beside that, on the mirrorless stucco wall another version of herself appeared—as an adult with fuller features.

When she moved, the girl and woman reflections moved with her in synchronization, and when she smiled the same teeth showed in both reflected smiles, without perceptible change from teen to adult.

She leaned close to the adult reflection, saw a long scar behind one eyebrow that she didn't have now, a scar that didn't appear on the teen reflection, and this gave her pause for thought.

I'm going to be injured.

Nonetheless she wanted to grow into that woman in her future, into that kindly countenance that gazed back upon her with the expression of mother to child. Emily didn't want to be a teenager any longer, not in this house with Victoria.

Nonna had told her that the teens were difficult years anyway, from physical and chemical changes in the body. But Nonna put an upbeat tone to it, adding that breezes still blew and birds sang and flowers grew and girls turned into young women despite the pain.

Emily had a sudden desire to call her grandparents and tell them she and Thomas were back. They must have worried terribly at their disappearance, as much as Emily's father. She wanted to go straight to their house and sit close by Nonna and talk to her about the Chalk Man and Squick and the power she had and the terrible occurrences in Squick's building.

Nonna would listen to her, wouldn't say she was crazy.

The wall and mirror images faded before her, and unbidden Ch'Var memories spilled forth, a dark cloud of indecipherable alien information that drifted over her, touching her and receding, touching and receding.

Each touch was heavier than the one previous, and she cried out words in an alien tongue that were not quite clear to her in meaning.

Then a voice asked, "What's the matter?" and she saw Thomas in the doorway, face flushed from his bath, his bare feet poking out beneath his robe.

"Nothing."

He sat on the cedar chest at the end of her bed, crossed his arms and frowned thoughtfully. "It's about all the stuff that happened to us, isn't it? Like you activating the Chalk Man and that deranged, strange guy, Peenchay, that you killed."

"That *I* killed?"

"Sure. You created the blackboard monster. Look, Sis, don't get riled at me. I don't wanna mess with you."

She scowled, but when she saw the bemused expression on his face and the twinkle in his eyes she couldn't suppress a smile and a little laugh. "It all happened, didn't it?" she said. "We didn't imagine it. Thomas, I'm frightened of the power. I don't know how to control it. What if I hurt someone accidentally, like you or Dad?"

Thomas considered this for a moment, his head tilted back in a thoughtful pose. Presently he replied, "You wouldn't. You couldn't. I see it this way. We were in the middle of a war, and Peenchay would have killed us if we didn't get him first."

"I didn't want to kill anyone," she said, her voice faltering, "not even that monster. I'm different from other kids, Thomas. I'd only suspected it before, but the extent is becoming clearer. I've got things rolling around in my head I don't understand, frightening things about Ch'Vars and Gweens and Nebulons, and . . . I just saw a flash . . . billions of faces, zillions of them at once. Squick did something to my mind with his filthy Nebulons, I'm not sure what.''

"I don't think we'll find any of this in Dad's medical books. I don't think it's hormones or . . ." He paused, and his eyes opened wide. "What about poltergeists, those noisy ghosts that make furniture fly and stuff? Could you be tied in with them?''

Emily laughed. "It's a better explanation than any I have, but the Chalk Man wasn't that noisy—except when he was chewing . . . eeuuu! It doesn't seem real. Do you know I can't even call you Tom-Tom anymore because of Squick calling you that? That evil man has taken something away from us, something that was precious and we'll never have again.''

"I'll get rid of the T-shirt.''

Emily nodded. "We're growing up in a hurry, I guess. Hey, you'd better finish dressing before Victoria starts yelling about something. She hasn't changed.''

"I wish she had,'' Thomas said. He traipsed across the hall to his room.

A few minutes later, satisfied she'd done the best she could with her appearance, Emily started down the stairs. A scream from below hurried her on her way. She wasn't sure, but the voice sounded something like Mrs. Belfer's, a loud, frightened cry that subsided quickly.

Emily raced through the house, past the kitchen to the housekeeper's quarters. Inside the back porch room, Victoria stood with outstretched arms, dancing a peculiar ballet with Mrs. Belfer. The housekeeper's red wig dangled from one side of her head, and she looked limp, a drunken rag doll. Mrs. Belfer's feet were dragging on the ground, and Emily noticed a scarf around her neck, with one of Victoria's long arms around the woman's neck, long fingers tight on the scarf.

"My God, you're killing her!" Emily shouted, and she pummeled her stepmother with her fists. "Let go of her, you witch, let her go!"

The scarf loosened to a large loop and Mrs. Belfer's head slid through. She slumped to the floor. Scarf still held in her outstretched hands, Victoria turned her attention to Emily. The fabric made crisp sounds as the woman stretched and released it—snap, snap, snap.

Emily hesitated. Should she call forth the Chalk Man? It would be so easy to eliminate Victoria from her life forever. Concentrating, Emily saw her protector's dim outline begin to sketch itself beside Victoria.

But Emily's father loved this woman, and the girl wasn't sure she could destroy someone he loved. Besides, Emily knew that she wanted this woman dead and out of her life forever, and the feelings were deep, a loathing so intense that it made the act terribly wrong. The Chalk Man's image began to fade.

"Dance with me," whispered Victoria, and she looped the scarf around Emily's neck.

Emily struggled in her grasp, felt the scarf bite into her neck, twisting against her skin until it threatened to cut off air. Victoria's eyes blazed with feral lavender light.

"Don't do this," Emily said. But she slid toward unconsciousness with the eyes of the woman luminous above her, a pair of unrelenting lavender suns. Emily couldn't believe her stepmother would kill her, not this debutante trained in the most exclusive finishing schools, this social butterfly who spoke civilized French and had the finest table manners.

They didn't strangle people in finishing school.

Emily slipped further into unconsciousness, and

she felt too weak to call for her Chalk Man. She sensed another presence nearby—in Victoria's blazing eyes?

Something in the eyes shocked Emily to awareness. They were red now, not lavender, and light bounced in the air in front of her eyes, like embers from a fire. The pressure on Emily's neck ceased, and the light expanded until it covered Victoria's face, concealing it. As quickly as it had expanded it contracted and became a dot of color, a single ember, burning brightly on the end of Victoria's nose.

Then the ember vanished, leaving only Victoria's startled face. She stared at Emily with eyes no longer filled by alien light, eyes that were lavender but without vitality. The scarf slipped from her hands and her arms dropped limply at her sides.

Slowly, Emily backed away, and her stepmother stood in one place as though stunned. Her perfect mouth opened and a babble of sound came forth in French and English, senseless ravings, without emotion.

Emily retrieved the scarf from the floor and tied Victoria's hands tightly behind her back. Victoria did not resist, hardly twitched a muscle.

Mrs. Belfer stirred and groaned, and Emily crouched beside her.

"What the hell . . . ." Mrs. Belfer said in a raspy voice. She rubbed a red mark that ringed her neck. "She tried to kill me."

With Emily's assistance the housekeeper sat up and stared angrily at Victoria. "What happened to her? She was all over me, I went under, and now she looks like a zombie."

"I don't know," Emily answered. "She acted like all her energy drained away, and I tied her up."

Mrs. Belfer forged all of her drunken facial wrinkles into a smile, and she gazed at Victoria. "How nice. Victoria, oh Victoria, did this little kid whip you? Tsk, tsk, look at you now.''

"Don't provoke her,'' Emily said. "She went into some kind of trance, and if she comes out of it she could get free.''

"Why does she keep standing there like that?''

Emily shrugged. "I don't know.''

"I'm gonna call your dad and get him home right away.''

"I called and left a message,'' Emily said. "He's in surgery. I'm sure he'll be home as soon as he can.''

"Well, when he shows up I got lots to tell him. This lady ain't what she's been puttin' on to be. Your dad had better watch out for you kids, and for himself. I don't blame you for runnin' away, but you gotta know there's terrible things happenin' out there in the world. Right now there's kids droppin' like flies with some god-awful disease that puts them into comas. You don't want that to happen.'' She straightened her shoulders and lifted her chin.

For a brief moment Emily saw the woman that Mrs. Belfer probably had been many years earlier, and felt a deep pity for her.

"I'm gonna call the cops,'' Mrs. Belfer said, and she punched one of the blue programmed buttons on the telephone.

Two policewomen escorted Victoria from the house. She went without protest to their blue and white patrol van while Emily and Mrs. Belfer watched.

"Acts like she's on something,'' one policewoman said as they eased Victoria onto a padded platform at the side of the van. "Custom drugs, maybe. The expensive stuff.''

"None o' that!'' Mrs. Belfer exclaimed. "She's

just nuts! And I got a lot more to tell you about her!'' And Mrs. Belfer winked at Emily.

Emily watched the platform slide into the back of the van, and she didn't feel the least bit smug or happy about Victoria's arrest. It would hurt Emily's father when he found out, and the girl wasn't sure what to tell him. What did Mrs. Belfer mean about more to tell?

Just before the van's side door slid shut, Emily saw a stream of tiny red lights fly out, and she was able to count them—seven—before they ascended out of sight. One—the first ember to appear—had been brighter than the others.

''Did you see that?'' Emily asked, glancing sidelong at Mrs. Belfer.

But the housekeeper seemed preoccupied with rubbing the wounds on her neck, and Emily didn't ask again.

CHAPTER TWENTY

> The end circles the beginning, and the
> sleeping Lordmother sleeps no more.
> —From a popular song

Guilt gnawed at Emily as she lay on her bed, staring at the circle of light made by her lamp on the ceiling. She'd spoken with her father too briefly that evening on the telephone. She'd told him she loved him, and he'd said the same of her and Thomas. He said he'd have to see to Victoria's situation before coming home.

"We'll wait up for you, Daddy," Emily had promised.

And she wondered what details she should give him. The sight of Victoria dull-eyed and unmoving had been shocking. Those funny specks of light that preceded Victoria's cessation of violence, had Emily brought those forth unknowingly? The thought that she might have done this muddled her sense of relief, sickened her.

She was free—rid of Squick, rid of Victoria and all the cruelty those people represented. Or was she? Emily felt like an instrument of destruction without controls—someone, or worse still, some thing—that couldn't be trusted around ordinary people, Gween or Ch'Var. The thought startled her. Who were the perpetrators of this or was it chance, a curious twisting of events? Did Squick or Jabu know the answers?

Thomas came into the bedroom. They sat cross-legged on the bed, talking, and Thomas smelled of soap he hadn't removed entirely from his hair, a sweet, clean odor that made life seem more familiar to Emily.

They decided the real story of their disappearance would sound too bizarre, that it should be adjusted, made palatable for adult ears. The best action seemed to be the worst. They'd have to tell a lie. One that would sound logical without getting them into too much trouble. Between them they decided what to say, and when the story was nearly perfect, Emily heard her father downstairs, talking in loud, anxious tones with Mrs. Belfer.

Thomas jumped to his feet, but Emily asked him to wait because of the yelling that had started downstairs.

The children listened.

Dr. Harvey was angry over Mrs. Belfer's failures, and he talked about a serious medical situation, mental damage to Victoria. Mrs. Belfer was overwhelming him with information he didn't seem prepared to hear, about a kid who'd died at one of Victoria's college parties, about a cover-up and videotape evidence, about a pact Mrs. Belfer and Victoria had entered into, a pact that deceived Dr. Harvey and the children. Mrs. Belfer was sobbing, she was so remorseful, and Emily felt sorry for her despite the revelations.

Presently Dr. Harvey stood in the doorway of the bedroom, curly hair puffed out at the sides, his eyes dark with emotion. The children embraced him, one on each side.

They sat atop the bed, the three of them, and Emily's father placed an arm around her shoulders. "Did you run away, Em?" he asked.

"I heard the ridiculous things she said to you on the telephone after we got home, that she could see lies all over my face. Well, I'm not a liar. I'm not the crazy one!'' Emily took a deep breath. "I'm sorry.'' She didn't say anything about Victoria's attempt on her.

"We didn't run away,'' Thomas said. "We went to visit someone.''

"I want the truth,'' Dr. Harvey said. "From the beginning.''

And Thomas told the story as they'd composed it, that they'd left the house early in the morning—before Mrs. Belfer was up. That they had decided to hike to their grandparents' but had become lost and ended up in a park the first night.

Dr. Harvey placed a hand on his forehead and rubbed vigorously. "It's almost eighty klicks to your grandparents' house. You both know how long it takes to drive that distance. How could you hope to walk it?''

"We weren't thinking straight,'' Emily said with a shrug. She wondered if he could feel the Great Lie, from his arm on her quivering shoulders. At least it was a white lie, one that didn't hurt anyone.

"We didn't have enough money to buy bus tickets for both of us the whole distance,'' Thomas said, improvising well. "After getting lost and sleeping in the park we wandered around the next day, and pretty soon we decided it would be best to come on home, but it was too late for that, so we slept in a highway rest stop the second night, under an overhang by a big map.''

"We forgot when you'd be back from your trip,'' Emily said, "and we didn't think Mrs. Belfer would notice.''

"I can't leave you with her anymore,'' Dr. Harvey said. "Especially now, with what she's said and what's happened to Victoria. I can't believe Victoria tried to kill her. But Mrs. Belfer's neck is red. What a sordid business.''

Again Emily resisted mentioning the attack on her,

and in an apparent mind-joining, Thomas said nothing of it either.

"I have this Mexico project I have to go to," Dr. Harvey said, "hundreds of peasants needing surgery. What a rotten time for this mess to hit."

"We're sorry, Daddy," Emily said.

"I know you are," he said. "I shouldn't have stayed with Victoria so long, don't know what madness came over me to make me do that. Love, I thought, but now I know better. I had called my lawyer and told him to file for divorce just before she went crazy. I guess I'll proceed with that. It's for the best. I thought I'd lost both of you. I had this terrible fear you were dead, lying out in the cold with no one caring. The police didn't seem to have any leads."

"We hiked a few kilometers after sleeping at the rest stop," Thomas said, "then caught a bus into town, and we barely had enough money for a cab to bring us home the rest of the way."

"And you didn't even leave a note for Mrs. Belfer? To let her know where you were headed?"

"No," Thomas said.

"It doesn't matter now. You're back, and that's the important thing." He held the children's hands in his own, and his touch was warm to Emily, a reassuring strength.

She clung to her father's hand. If only the truth about where they had been didn't defy reality. If only she understood what the truth represented.

He spoke of Mexico, that it would require a year's leave of absence, that the project involved building a hospital as well as his medical assistance and teaching program. And he mentioned the need for a nanny to take care of the children.

"Can we go live with Nonna and Panona?" Emily asked.

Dr. Harvey thought for a while, while Emily gazed

alternately at him and at the shadow of his head on
the wall, from the light of the lamp. "They're too
old," he said, "can't keep up with you kids."

"You'd be surprised," Thomas said. "Can we
please?"

"We know some kids at the school there," Emily
said, "neighbors we've played with. It's nice there."

"I'll think about it," Dr. Harvey said. "And even
if I agree to ask them, it's not a sure thing. Nonna
and—"

"Oh, they'll say yes!" Emily said. "I know they
will."

The next morning, Nonna and Panona drove to
the house, and a tearful reunion was had, full of
hugs and good cheer. The elderly couple agreed to
take the children.

A doctor called from the hospital that morning
and reported to Emily's father that Victoria was almost coherent, and in all likelihood she would recover fully. Over breakfast the Harveys discussed the
medical and criminal travails facing Victoria, and
Dr. Harvey had second thoughts about the timing of
his divorce, not wishing to aggravate his wife's condition.

"I still have feelings for her," he admitted.

He decided to delay the proceedings until Victoria
regained her strength, until she could cope with the
leavings of her life. But he would go through with it
eventually, he promised. And he spoke of an excellent alcohol-rehabilitation facility he would encour-
age Mrs. Belfer to use, at his expense.

From the kitchen table, Emily saw the light on in
the back porch room, and occasionally Mrs. Belfer
walked by the window facing the porch. She was up
quite early for her, in a bright green "Sunday dress"
that Emily had not seen in a long time.

My life is falling into place, Emily thought. *And so is hers. She'll be fine.*

Emily and Thomas ate the equivalent of five breakfasts between them, from a count Panona made of the items consumed, and all had a good laugh over this. Emily overflowed with happiness. It was wonderful to be with her family again. But a small lingering doubt hung over her pleasure, like a rain cloud about to release its bombs of water. No matter how she tried to shake herself loose from the cloud, it hung there nevertheless—waiting to inundate her.

The children moved to their grandparents' house that afternoon.

In the basement bedroom the children shared there, after they had gone to bed and the house was stilled by the softness of night, Emily talked with Thomas about their decision. They had separate beds, and light came from a night-light stuck in the wall outlet between their beds. It was a bright plastic kitten face illuminating the darkness, and Emily thought of the plastic kitten broken from the door handle of the room in Squick's building. She'd lost the kitten somewhere in the excitement, but assured herself that it would be all right. It was the only thing she missed from that awful place.

"I hope Daddy isn't unhappy with us," she said. "We didn't even ask to go to Mexico with him."

"I don't think he wanted us to. There's lots of sickness in the jungle, and he doesn't want us to get any of it. Probably danger where he's going, too. This way he'll have less worries."

"I suppose you're right. Thomas, promise you'll always stay with me no matter what."

"That's a screwball thing to say. Of course I will. You're my sister."

"I mean, no matter what, no matter how crazy I might get. The stuff in my head is still bothering me, still stirring around, and I don't know how to deal with it, I don't know what it's doing to me.''

"You're just trying to scare me."

"No, I'm not. I'm telling you everything I can, because you're the only person in the whole wide world who should know this stuff. We can't even tell Nonna and Panona about it.''

"I think we could. They're not like other adults."

"Maybe, but you and I have a bond, like nothing we've ever imagined. I can't put it into words." Her voice lowered, and she said, "They're watching us. I'm sure of it. Whoever they are, they're here.''

She saw her brother looking at her from just outside his covers, his eyes open wide. "They?"

Something trembled on the edge of Emily's consciousness, a faint whisper of what was yet to come. "Ch'Vars and Gweens are fighting for control inside me," she said. "And the Ch'Vars are winning. They're killing parts of me.''

A shudder ran along the length of her spine.

CHAPTER TWENTY-ONE

In darkness there is always light, for the
one feeds upon the other.
—From the ancient
Ch'Var "Riddle Song"

Emily had been counting showers since moving in
with her grandparents, and this was her third. She
nudged a brass lever to shut off the water, grabbed
a towel and stepped gingerly onto the bath mat.

She was on the main floor, with the small frosted
bathroom window swung open, revealing the bright,
variant greens of trees, and filtered morning sun.
She felt she had returned to life, a glorious feeling.

As she dried herself she caught a glimpse of
something in the mirror beneath a frosty layer of
condensation—little red sparks of light. A trick of
sunlight?

But the mirror was on the same wall with the window. Could it be light bouncing off the glass of the
shower door?

The sparks became clearer, sharper, and like fish
swimming to the surface they seemed to be drawing
nearer. Fascinated, Emily stopped drying herself and
watched. They were hypnotic, dancing lights, one
brighter than the others, like the lights she had seen
around Victoria, the lights that sped from the police
van after the arrest.

Abruptly the lights emerged from the mirror surface into the room—separate little glowdots with one

still larger. A sensation of numbness crept over Emily's body.

She grew cold, shivered, and wrapped herself in the towel, then edged back against the shower door. The lights were between her and the door, forming a barrier to escape. She considered dodging under them and lunging for the door handle, but hesitated.

Emily feared the lights.

The brightest became larger, more brilliant, and a bearded face appeared within it, filtered by a mist. She recognized Director Jabu.

"We have much to discuss," Jabu said. Six small red lights danced at the sides of his face.

"Here?" Emily asked. "Now? I'm wrapped in a towel." She pulled the towel closer.

"You are obligated to consider matters more important than personal comfort or modesty. You are an alpha-mother, the mitochondrial progenitor of a new human race. I sense that you are not aware of everything, and there is much you need to know. Not only for the sake of your own race, but for—"

"You're in my bathroom. Get out!"

"Respectfully, I decline. For your own good, for the good of your people, for the good of my people."

"Did you see me naked?"

"No."

"But your light . . . it was . . ."

Jabu smiled gently. "Please don't worry. I was in transit, and in that mode saw nothing but the filament of fire I travel on."

"What is all this gibberish? And where is your body?"

"Forget such concerns. Please. Let me talk."

Emily, noting a deferential tone, wrapped the towel tighter around herself, securing it with a tuck. She stared at Jabu. His face was flat, of two dimensions only, but the eyes seemed different, in a realm of their own. They were dark and moist, with slight, even gaps all the way around each, as if the eyes were not in contact with the rest of his face.

"I'm conserving energy by not materializing completely in human form," he said. "These other embers are my associates. I've brought them a long way."

"I'd like to get dressed," Emily said.

"There's time for that, but first you owe me a favor. I saved you from your stepmother. You saw the lights around her?"

"Yes! That was you? You went inside her head?"

"And made her, ah, temporarily crazy." A smile twitched at the edges of his mouth. "Ironic, isn't it? As I recall from amoeba-cam reports, your stepmother thought you were the loony one."

"I don't find that amusing."

"You wouldn't. Alpha-mothers are very compassionate, you know."

"What's this alpha-mother you keep babbling about?"

"I see fear in your expression, fear of the changes that are occurring within you, fear of what lies ahead. You're aware of something happening to you internally, but you aren't quite sure of what it is. I can help you understand."

Emily took a deep breath, let it out slowly.

"You're the first of a new race," Jabu said. "If you live, the race lives. If you perish, the race perishes."

"How do you know this?"

"I got medical reports on you and your brother. We tracked your family DNA."

He explained to the astounded girl that she and Thomas were fraternal twins, that the boy had been born years after her of a delayed egg, and that this only happened in the rare historical instances of alpha-mothers and their brothers. Jabu told her of

Mother Ch'Var, of Ch'Vars and Gweens, of Lord-mother's Way, and of Mother Ch'Var's delayed twin, Brother Epan. And Jabu spoke of the Nebulons his race could not live without.

Emily forgot her concerns about modesty, and to her the words of this strange, bearded head rolled across flat lips, from a realm that wasn't quite her own. But his words rang true and vibrant, as if she had known these things all along, as if they had been unexamined objects from a shelf of her mind.

"Brother Thomas," Emily said softly. "Sounds kinda religious. Is that what this is all about, a new religion?"

"That's likely. There are many nuances of religion, as many variations as there are shades of color or tones of sound. No matter what you do, history shows that you will be beheld as a goddess, as we behold our glorious Lordmother."

"With every new race? What about the Gweens?"

"It is said that they too had a Lordmother and a Way of the Lordmother, but that it fell into disarray with time."

"What if I don't want to play the part? What if none of the others in my race know an alpha-mother even exists?"

The flat face showed surprise. "Possible, I suppose. But why would you wish to do that? We adore our Lordmother. She is inspiration for us, salvation when times are difficult."

"I . . . it's just that I don't know if I believe you, or if I can handle all the responsibility if what you say is true. I'm scared."

"You'll grow into the job, you'll learn to accept your future. Give it time. Alpha-mothers have certain . . . powers. You've noticed yours?"

"Well, I've always had a vivid imagination that enabled me to visualize wild, wonderful things. When that monster Peenchay came after us, I con-

jured up a protector. My protector swallowed Peenchay and spat him out, what was left of him. It was
horrible.''

"I saw the result. I assure you we do not condone
Peenchay's behavior. He was an aberration, an
abomination carried over from ancient times, another flaw in our race.''

"Thomas helped me mindshape the protector. He
knew I could do it.''

"That is the way of the First Brother. He is growing into his powers, too, and they will complement
your own. Often he will become aware of circumstances earlier than you and will guide you.''

Jabu's eyes seemed full of concern, and he
warned, "Be careful with your powers. It is said that
every alpha-mother has different abilities, and history is no predictor of these specifics. You have one
that worries me more than a little—I feel it now. You
possess a certain sensuality that's difficult for a man
to escape. Myself, Squick, probably others." His
eyes closed for a moment. "I fear for you.''

Emily felt her face flush. "Will my race weaken
inevitably, as yours has? Will we have an Achilles'
heel such as your Nebulons?''

"So many variables. I cannot say." The eyes
seemed to penetrate the heart of Emily, and she felt
uncomfortable, invaded.

She saw a vulnerability in the eyes, beyond their
strength, and she understood this. "The Nebulons
are not dead," she said impulsively. The realization
made her short of breath, and she added, "I have
them, all of them . . . in my body.''

"I wondered about that, and whether you would
admit it.''

"There might be a way to release them. I don't
know.''

"Return with me, Lordmother Emily, and I will
make certain you are safe. Homaal, where I come

from, is a fortress. My race depends upon your safety.''

And if the Nebulons are released? Emily thought. *What then?* She couldn't get a full reading on this man, not from the fragments evident to her thus far.

"Tell me the whole truth," Emily said. She looked at the lights dancing beside Jabu, watched them flit about, never going far away, always staying within a few centimeters of Jabu's apparition.

"My associates, you mean?"

"Begin with them."

"I'm sorry. Five are members of my Inventing Corps. They can't see or hear you, and only bits of my speech are entering their auditory sensors. I brought them along to examine you firsthand, in case you weren't cooperative. I sense, however, that you understand my concerns, that you are sympathetic."

Sympathetic? Yes, I suppose I am.

"And your sixth associate?" Emily inquired.

"You don't miss anything, do you? That's Squick, but not the old Squick. He's changed. He's better now. Uh . . .''

"And?"

"Uh, he has your brother's embidium. The childhood memories of your brother are stitched seamlessly with Squick's own, and have soothed Squick's troubled spirit. Your brother is fine, a phenomenon I don't understand. The extraction didn't . . .''

"Because of the powers of Brother Thomas? It sounds strange, calling him that."

"You'll get used to it. His powers . . . yes, perhaps. We meant him no harm. It was part of the system to extract from him, a very old system, Lordmother's Way. Should I tell you more? I can speak of Squick's motives, of shittah, of anything you wish.''

"Calm yourself, Jabu. I'll talk with you, I'll work

with you. But I won't go with you to Homaal. I'm staying with my grandparents.''

"Not practical, and might not be safe here. We must devote all our energies to the problem at hand, beginning with restoration of the Nebulons.''

"I'm not leaving my grandparents.''

"You must face your responsibilities!''

Emily's gaze burned through the mists that surrounded Jabu, and she saw him flinch. "I have no responsibility to you,'' she said, "not after what your people have done to Gweenchildren. Call upon your own Lordmother. Raise her from the dead and undo the harm your kind have brought to Earth.''

Jabu's eyes became frantic. "We are not predators! There is much you need to understand, the therapeutic benefits to adults, the necessity of . . . deceit.''

Emily understood some of this, and to her this unfortunate man was beginning to look like a captive in a system he hadn't initiated.

"I admit to deceit very hesitantly,'' Jabu said. "You must realize that Gweens are perhaps even worse. Look at Gween politics, for example.''

"You are in no position to criticize.''

"Technically you may have abused your powers,'' Jabu snapped. Then his tone softened. "I'm not accusing you of anything. I'm sure it was unintentional, a defensive reaction. You are young, unfamiliar with your powers. But the results to our race are calamitous!''

"I did only what was necessary to survive. Your Nebulons intruded upon me. They weren't invited, you had no right!''

"How did you decide what to do? How did you— where in your body are they?'' The head twitched with agitation.

Emily could not answer any of this. She had only a vague recollection of the attempted extraction and a lingering sense of tremendous fear and violence over the moment.

"There will be changes," she said presently, and her voice attained a depth of tone that astonished her. "For days that will seem like years to you, I will consider everything, taking your needs into account. When I have organized my thoughts into neat columns and rows, when I have absorbed all that has happened, there will be new directions. Never again will Gweenchildren be left comotose and helpless. Nor will they be abused in ways I find too loathsome to repeat."

Jabu appeared to be confused.

"I know you thought you were doing right for your people," she said. "But there are others to consider. Gweens have rights, too. Maybe my people, my new race, will police or monitor the situation, creating an atmosphere in which all humans can live in peace."

"But we must make extractions. They're critical, don't you understand? Even the comotose part is unavoidable. Other matters I'm sure we can work out."

"Thomas avoided coma."

"But only because of who he is."

"There is a secret there nonetheless, something to be learned from his experience. A way to prevent suffering."

Jabu told her of the researches of his Inventing Corps, and Emily was heartened by this. But Jabu did not appear heartened. His was a dismal countenance to behold, a picture of dejection.

"What will you name your people?" he asked.

"Maybe I'll let them name themselves. Or maybe they won't know they're different. I'll see."

"May I remain near you?" Jabu asked, his tone subdued. "To answer questions, to provide more information? I will tell no lies, will conceal nothing from you. Time is of the essence, and if we can speed the process in any way . . . do you think it would be all right?''

"If you wish. You can find a place safe from detection?''

"Do you have a little hand mirror?''

"Why, yes. In the cabinet under this sink.''

"Mirrors are suitable places of concealment, even cracked ones. We can burrow deep into the light crevices within the glass, can rest there in our ember form. There are many mysteries about mirrors . . . much I can tell you one day . . . much yet for you to learn.''

"And for you," Emily said.

Jabu looked abashed.

"Though I allow you to remain nearby," Emily said, "remember my powerful protector. Remember what he did to Peenchay."

"I won't oppose you." The flat face became a glowing red ember, a fat dot of light. It formed a line with the others, and they disappeared neatly into a crack between the doors under the sink.

Emily sighed and began to consider the future of humankind. She saw herself at the nexus of all civilization, of all sentient life, and through Jabu's eyes she gazed across the ice plain toward the horizon. She felt very old, much older than the birthday she was about to have.

EPILOGUE

When at long last the young alpha-mother beheld the
great fortress of Homaal, it is said that a susurration
of sound escaped her lips. "This is my Revelation,"
she said. "I am the Alpha and the Omega, who is,
who was, and who will always be."

ABOUT THE AUTHORS

Brian Herbert, son of Frank Herbert (creator of *Dune*), sold his first story in 1981, then began a highly successful writing career which has led to both critical acclaim and commercial success. His novels include *The Race for God, Sudanna, Sudanna, Man of Two Worlds* (written with his father), and *Prisoners of Arionn*. Brian has at one time or other worked as a book salesman, an insurance agent, the chief financial officer for a clothing company, and a real estate investment manager. He now makes his home in Redmond, Washington, with his wife and three children.

Marie Landis has worked as a free-lance writer for more than a decade and has published numerous short stories. A few years ago, after more than thirty years of separation, she and her cousin Brian Herbert reunited and decided to write a novel (her first): *Memorymakers*. Marie has worked as a labor arbitrator, an assistant city manager, a reporter, a commercial artist, and a cryptographer. She makes her home in Mercer Island, Washington, with her husband and a cat named Orson.

THE NOVARIAN SOCIETY

An organization of readers who appreciate the books of Brian Herbert is now being established. Called ''The Novarian Society'' (based upon concepts in his critically acclaimed novel *The Race For God*), the club is an information center about Brian Herbert's books, strongly held beliefs and public appearances.

Newsletters are published on a quarterly basis, and presently there are no membership dues. For more information, please send a self-addressed stamped envelope to:

**The Novarian Society
93 Pike Street, Suite 308
Seattle, WA 98101**